The Boy Who Fell to Earth

by Wayne Kyle Spitzer

2

own copy. Thank you for respecting the hard work of this
author.

Part One

3

Chronoscope | 1966—1972

HE LIVES in Spokane, Washington, a smudge of town just off the railway, a place rust-brown by day and elm-dark by night, filled with grain elevators and dim orange streetlamps; a place still without a freeway even in the late '60s. His immediate family consists of a mother and father, both in their forties, a brother, who is three years older, and himself. Because he is the youngest of seven boys—four from his mother's first marriage and a still-born between he and his brother—everyone calls him 'the Kid.'

They have a ritual which begins at the Phillips 66, in the late afternoon or twilight, where his mother buys him and his brother Cokes and candy cigarettes—Cokes in tall, swirly glass bottles, candy cigarettes in delicate cellophane wrappers. Often she buys them comic books—she calls them 'funny books'—such as *Porky Pig* and *Daffy Duck,* picked from a tall newsstand that squeaks when rotated. He is enchanted by their covers,

5

by the slick, glossy paper and vivid colorizations, the pictures between filmy, rough-edged pages that he can follow, and in a sense, 'read.' But what affects him the most, what he wants most to know better, are those things he can see and touch and hear but not read—the marks laid out in tidy rows within the body of the pictures; the roll of the cash register's tumbler as his mother pays for the books; the runes ticking past on the gas pump as his father fills the tank.

"Thirty-six cents a gallon," his father always says, shaking his head.

"And 10 cents for a funny book!" says his mother.

Then, as father turns the key and they rattle onto the road in the old Chevy work truck, Elvis takes over, singing "Suspicious Minds."

And they go *riding*.

THEY RIDE EVERYWHERE, but he can only imagine what goes on in the farmhouses and the office buildings they pass. He imagines that technicians, who work underground in cramped rooms—rooms full of control panels and television screens—operate traffic lights. That they go in and out through manholes and work down

6

there day and night. He imagines them in gray coveralls with patches on the sleeves—three solid circles, red, yellow, and green. He imagines that *The Creature from the Black Lagoon* was filmed in Spokane's Manito Park, on a boat in Mirror Lake, across from his grandmother's house, and that manhole covers steam because the traffic technicians' rooms—like those of the submarine on *Voyage to the Bottom of the Sea*—are pressurized.

But the ride is not always wonderful. When his parents buy a Ford station wagon in 1970 the family celebrates by going to an all-you-can-eat Chinese buffet, where he gorges himself on cheese mussels, which he loves but cannot digest. He christens the new car by vomiting all over its rear storage compartment, the result of which is a carpet of cheese-mussel vomit—drying on the upholstery, and on the groceries, cracking. His mother thinks it is an isolated case of motion sickness, brought on by the excitement of the new car, and by loving cheese mussels too much. They pull over at a Phillips 66 station where she cleans it all up.

Because the wagon has a back seat he starts bringing along his Marx play-sets—Marx's Prehistoric Scenes, Marx's Modern Farm, Marx's Service Station, Marx's

Cape Kennedy, all in tin cases with vinyl handles, like attachés. He opens them on his lap, unfolding new worlds—worlds filled with fences and tractors and service stations, but also cycad trees, dinosaurs, Saturn V rockets—four-color comic book worlds of cyan, magenta, yellow, and black.

One afternoon they are riding along Trent Avenue when the light of the setting sun is blocked by an enormous sheet-metal building. The building looks like an aircraft hangar and bears a massive logo high above its daylight windows—sleek yellow letters on a starry black field—like the titles at the beginning of *Star Trek*.

It is obvious to him that this is where they film the show. He supposes they have the entire ship in there, illuminated by huge lights, supported by lattices of scaffolding. For the first time he thinks of the future— not his future, not tomorrow or the next day or the day after—the future, a future colored Astronaut White, Galaxy Gold, and Re-entry Red. A future his mother and father say will be here before he knows.

I | The Sound of Trouble

HE IS SITTING at the dining room table before a long, low window, building plastic model kits with his brother, when he first hears it—a rumbling and a snarling, coming up the road, coming closer to their house. Out of the corner of his eye he sees a ghostly white blur, a car, swoop into the driveway. Its headlights dazzle his vision as it draws closer to the window. He watches their beams move across the schematics spread over the table— lighting up the *U.S.S. Enterprise*'s saucer section, still attached to its mold, setting the ship's cigar-shaped secondary hull on fire, key- lighting its long, tubular warp nacelles. The beams sets the tap water to shimmer in a little porcelain bowl, where strips of red and gold decals float. They glint off the edge of an orange-white tube of Testors glue. Then they're gone.

He looks out the window, nimbuses of light still imprinted on his eyes. In their place sits the car, headlamps cooling, fading to black, plumes of exhaust rising. It is long and low and Astronaut white. Its driver's door swings open, as he has seen the hatch of the Apollo spacecraft swing open after splashdown. His father emerges, dressed in his baggy white paint clothes: his

9

hair is greased back, his face tanned; he is wearing aviator glasses—an astronaut returned to earth.

The Kid doesn't say anything, just watches as his dad's paint truck swings into the drive behind the car. Out climbs Fast Eddy, also still in his paint clothes. He is smoking a cigarette and carrying a can of Olympia beer. "The man is 40 going on 60," his mother once described him on the phone, "but is our star employee." His father says Fast Eddy can double-coat the interior of a medium-sized home in less than a work day, all by himself.

"Hey, Eddy!" shouts his brother. He gets up and hurries out, the screen door banging behind him.

The Kid follows, gluey fingertips sticking to the schematics, causing them to swish from the table, spilling the model's pieces. There is a click as the bathroom door is unlatched. He pauses at the screen, looking over his shoulder.

His mother stands bolt upright, looking beyond him at the car. She is buttoning her blouse with one hand, holding a small mirror in the other. Her face has been tanned over the summer, her dark-blonde hair bleached gold; still she seems blanched, her expression blank. She reminds him of the astronaut in *2001: A Space Odyssey,*

10

Bowman, after passing through the Star Gate—paralyzed, transformed. A man his mother described as having just seen it all, "the beginning, the end, *everything.*"

She sets the mirror down and steadies herself against the table. Her expression softens. She doesn't quite shine, as would be typical, but something replaces the mask; something in the eyes only, something akin to her true self—something warm, blush, living.

"Go on ahead," she says. "I'll pick that up."

And she smiles—sweetly, wanly.

THE BOYS RACE out to the car amidst a September sunset—the Kid, now six, and his brother, now nine.

They circle the car in opposite directions as it idles in the pre-twilight, the brother laughing, hollering out, the Kid tentative, silent, speculative.

"S-S!" shouts the brother, "It's an *S-S!*"

"Sheldon Spitzer, how about that?" says Fast Eddy.

"Right," chuckles the brother. "Try Super Sport."

The Kid completes his circuit, stares at the black-accented grill and the chromed 'S-S' indicia centered

11

there. He can't yet read but recognizes the shapes. *S-S.* As in *U.S.S.* As in not just car. As in *Enterprise.*

His father opens the passenger's side door, gestures to him like Bob Barker on *The Price is Right.* "...a brand-new car!"

A big teenager who lives next door lopes across the field, arms swinging. "Just about," he drawls. Everyone calls him B.B.—because his name is 'Billy,' and because he walks like Bigfoot. "1968—five years old. Nice El Camino."

"El Camino," repeats the Kid. He steps close and stares in at the cab: at the chromed shifter and radio and the futuristic speedometer and council clock; at the single black bench seat and the flesh-colored carpeting—which rises, in the middle of the floor, to meet the shifter's rubber baffling. He hardly notices his brother opening the driver's door and slipping behind the wheel. He hardly notices anything but the carpeted floor and the sumptuous mound, which together form a hammock, almost, beneath the dashboard's black, enveloping shelter.

"Where the heck is everyone going to sit?" says his brother, rocking the wheel, pretending to drive. The

12

dome light causes a queer play of shadows over his face, teasing out features the Kid, the very mirror of their father, does not possess.

"Oh, I'll just ride in the back," drawls B.B.

"There's plenty of room for everyone," says his father. "You're not that big yet."

"I will be," says the brother. He pulls a handle under the dash, pops the hood.

The Kid doesn't say anything, only peers through the rear window at the payload bay, which takes the place of back seats.

His father has purchased a white 1968 El Camino with a black vinyl roof and matching decals, but *he* sees a spaceship, an aerodynamic domicile: a *rocket* with twin-domed hood scoops and louvered ports and long, pin-striped rear quarter panels, like warp nacelles, which through an alchemy known to Federation engineers and certain boys and girls can fold space, can warp time.

They huddle around the engine compartment—Fast Eddy, father, Sheldon and B.B.—as he peers between, glimpses something black and chrome and complicated before his brother blocks the view—purposely, it seems.

13

He keeps trying to see as Fast Eddy talks like he paints, *fast.*

"It's not the cylinders themselves that move, see. It's the pistons. Each cylinder has a spark plug, which causes compressed gas to combust and re-combust—*bang-bang-bang,* like that. The sparks are timed so that they push the pistons down and drive the crankshaft…"

"How many cylinders?" asks the brother.

"Eight," says his father.

"Hah!" cries B.B. "Explains that!"

"Explains what?"

"The sound of trouble when you pulled in," says B.B.

The Kid is on the pavement, crawling between their legs. He figures if he can't see it from above he'll see it from below.

Fast Eddy says: "Huh? No, that's not the sound of trouble. That's glass packs. The sound of trouble is when something goes *wrong.*"

The Kid is on his back now. He is reaching up into the purring, whirring compartment, intending to pull himself farther under, when his father grabs him by both ankles, yanks him out.

14

"Aye, aye, aye!" he shouts. He pulls him to his feet, draws him away from the others. "You don't *ever* reach into machinery like that. Not ever, Buddy!"

He looks at his father numbly, feeling foolish beyond words. He knows that Sheldon and Fast Eddy and B.B. are looking at him also, but does not return their gaze.

His father massages his shoulders and points him toward the field, to where his Styrachosaurus model sits like an ornament on the old Ford wagon. "Someone's going to make off with that," he says.

He focuses on it, squinting in the setting sun. His father gives him a nudge. He runs after his model.

GRASSHOPPERS SCATTER, ticking and whirring, as he moves through the field. He picks the model up off the hood of the wagon—one of its legs falls off, tumbling into the grass, which is knee-high, golden. He picks it up and examines it. The breeze tosses his hair. He looks past the green, pebble-textured model part—at the old Ford station wagon. Although he rode in it only yesterday, the light- brown car looks as though it has been here forever, merged with the grass and weeds—as though it were

15

already receding from him, from the family. He looks at the *new* car, at his father and brother and B.B. and Fast Eddy. He opens the driver's door of the wagon, watching them, and sits in the doorframe.

He tries to fit the Styrachosaur's leg back onto its body, but discovers that the little plastic knob that holds it in place is broken. The breeze blows and ruffles the grass. He looks at their new house, which is painted white with black accents, like his father's new car— thinks of his mother holding her hand-mirror. He does not know why he should think of this just now, or why the thought should bother him. His earlier notion of folding space and warping time seems suddenly threatening. There is something beneath the idea, something he can divine but not apprehend, a hidden layer.

His brother shouts, "Can I rev it? Can I rev it just once?"

"Hold on, Buddy," says their father. "Mary Lee! Let's go for a ride!"

The Kid fidgets. He waits for her to come out, feeling suddenly queasy, feeling as though she might in fact not come out—the fear is so alien that it seems to rise up in him like bile.

She emerges at last, wearing her fuzzy coat and carrying coats for his brother and himself: new coats, fresh as the paint on the new car, and the new house, and his father's job-sites—all the schools and grocery stores across Spokane his parents have bid on and won. "The boys have school tomorrow," she says, adding, "Where's the Kid?"

She looks around for him, spies him through the weeds. "What are you doing out there? Come join the party."

He wonders why he can't stop shaking. Why his stomach bucks and twists; why he's convinced the earth might suddenly fall away, the sun and moon blink out, the clouds roil black.

"Okay! Give her a rev!" shouts his father. The car's engine revs and roars.

The Kid leaps to his feet, startled. *Something* happens—it seems to him the universe itself just ignites and rolls over, right there, under his shoes. He falls down instantly, quaking and dry-heaving.

17

The car's engine roars and roars. "That's enough!" barks his father. Fast Eddy laughs.

The Kid coughs and spits and wipes his mouth. He is shaking uncontrollably. He peers through the grass and weeds, sees his mother hurrying toward him, her tanned face and blonde hair appearing gray in the waning sunlight. He gets up suddenly and runs toward her, his own blonde hair flying.

She has hardly finished stooping when he collides against her breast. "I—I was afraid—Bowman—how you said—I don't—I don't want...." He bursts into tears, presses into her coat.

She rocks him back and forth, patting his back. "There, there, Sweetie. Now, now."

He doesn't know what to say—what it is that he truly even feels. Something has brushed him, has *bruised* him.

"Something awful," he says.

"Shhh," she says. "There is nothing awful." She runs her hands over his hair, kisses his forehead. They remain that way for several minutes, saying nothing. At last she turns him away gently. "There's only that, see?"

She points to the setting sun, to the clouds shot through with red and gold.

He stares at them, sniffling. Suddenly everything seems perfect again—safe, spacious, mild. The air is cool, and fragrant with his mother's hairspray. He senses that she alone is interested in him; not his father, certainly not his brother—not his Sunday school teachers or the girls across the street. After awhile he says, "What if it goes out? What if—God turns it off?"

She plucks at his hair, straightens it out. "He turns it off every night. And what happens every morning?"

He swipes at his eyes, sniffs.

She retakes his shoulders gently in her hands, turns him back to face her. "What happens every morning?"

"He turns it back on again."

She smiles. "Which means it never really went out."

He stares at her as she releases his shoulders— slowly, delicately, as though she was balancing him on a wire. "My favorite Martian," she says. She tries to smooth his cowlicks, "Sensitive antennae and all." She laughs. "I don't know how we'll get through sometimes."

19

The Kid smiles, a bit awkwardly, then turns to look at the sun—sees the station wagon silhouetted against it. "It looks lonely out there," he says.

"It's just a car, Sweetie. It can't feel lonely." She places a hand on his shoulder, steering him away. "Besides, we have a new one now."

II | The Starlight

SHE LEADS HIM by the hand back to the El Camino. "Make room for your brother, Sheldon. Go stand by Ed."

Sheldon laughs, good-naturedly but not wholly sincere. "Oh, that's how we'll fit."

He goes and stands by Ed.

"I'll just go on back home, I guess," drawls B.B.

They form a semi-circle around the engine compartment, the sun dipping below the horizon—the Kid at the driver's side, standing on tip-toe, hands on the fender; Sheldon and Fast Eddy opposite, Mom and Dad at the grill. The tip of the sun casts long shadows across the pavement and over the engine compartment. Aside from the whirring of the engine and a handful of robins, there is complete silence, as though they are praying.

"What are we looking at?" his mother says softly.

The Kid listens, staring at the humming engine.

"About four years," says his father. "One-hundred-fifty dollars per month."

"Well...let's hope we win the community college bid," she says.

"We *will,* Mary Lee," says his father. He nods at the engine. "Pretty nice, don't you think? The boys can ride around in the back. And we can back in at the drive-in and put lawn chairs—"

She kisses his father's cheek, picks at a few locks of his hair. She doesn't seem to think much of the car, as a car, at all. "I think it will have to last us a long while," she says.

"She'll last," says Fast Eddy. He takes a swig of beer, sucks on his cigarette. "She's centered properly, see. It's nothing you can quantify. She's centered properly somewhere in her guts, so that everything radiating out from that is centered, too."

His mother sighs. Everybody else listens. They listen because in spite of being a high school drop-out and not having any front teeth, Fast Eddy knows stuff—not things, no details—*stuff.* Stuff that seems wise.

21

"What you get without that center is system failure," he says. "Sort of a Diaspora of parts, none of them connected and none of them functioning properly." He looks at the Kid suddenly, startling him a little. "But you have to listen for the sound of trouble, and if you hear it, you have to find it. It might be something really simple, something right at the surface, like a loose sparkplug cable. But it might be something deeper. Something you have to dig down to, or look at from another angle. Sometimes you just need some help, a precision instrument, say, like a full diagnostic scan, so you can see through the walls of things. And sometimes— sometimes you just have to cut her open. Cut her open and start peeling back the layers."

The Kid swallows, uncomfortable beneath his gaze. He looks down and watches the belts spin; smoothly, silkily, winding through cogs like water moccasins. He thinks of starting first grade at Broadway Elementary School the next day and of the summer now passed, and of all the stuff he loves; of hot-buttered popcorn at the Starlight Drive-in Theater, and 7-11 Slurpees in collectible cups—cups themed around muscle cars and sports teams, super heroes, movie monsters. He thinks of

22

the World Trade Center, tallest buildings on earth, completed the previous summer. Of Apollo 14 and Alan Shepard golfing on the moon—Apollo 15 coming up, and the deployment of the lunar rover. He wonders what it will be like to ride with his family across the moon someday.

"Okay, gang," his mother says, and claps her hands together—causing him to jump. "We're going to the Starlight. First show only—if it's okay with Dad."

"Might be our last chance," says Dad. "It's September. They'll be gone soon, all of them."

The Kid blinks. He looks up from the humming, whirring perfection of the engine, scans the faces of everyone around it: at Fast Eddy hunched over the opposite fender, cigarette dangling, paint-spattered bangs hanging; at Sheldon, pointing and questioning, interacting with the car and the people, looking and acting nothing like he does, at his mother, uncomfortable in her skin, interested in the car because his *father* is interested and she's in love with him; at his father, who pats and rubs her back, who is covered head to toe with multi-colored paint, and is not an astronaut…and back to his mother.

23

Who looks over at him, the last rays of the sun outlining her hair, and smiles.

GOING TO THE DRIVE-IN is nothing new; the brothers have been going since before they could walk. *Riding* there, in the back of the El Camino, with wind in their hair—twilit, October wind, carrying hints of musk and smoke, mystery, danger—*that's* new. For the Kid, who spends most of the ride lying upon his back, gazing at stars and the wing-lights of airplanes, at the canopies of leaves swishing overhead, it becomes even more—proof of something he has sensed but not seen: a new schema of life altogether, something previously hidden by the roof of the car, by his failure even to look. *The world from another angle,* as Fast Eddy might say.

The Starlight is surrounded by enormous high-tension towers, which dot the countryside all around it and are threaded with sagging power-lines, like cobwebs. The marquee reads:

"THE LEGEND OF BOGGY CREEK: A TRUE STORY"

24

PLUS   CO-HIT!   HUGH BEAUMONT "THE
MOLE PEOPLE"

ONLY $2 A CARLOAD!

The Kid and his brother stand behind the passenger compartment of the Camino, leaning against the rear window, hands spread on the black vinyl roof, as they pull up to the ticket kiosk. He watches a bill move from his father's hand to the attendant's—who pushes keys, causing the cash register to chime and its drawer to bang open. The numbers on the register's bar are a blur until they stop one by one—$2.00. The attendant puts the bill into the tray, bangs down the little metal clip—hands his father three ones. His fingers are dirty with what appears to be engine oil. He bangs shut the little window as his father pulls forward, the Camino's engine snarling, transaction completed, *bang, bang, bang,* like that.

The first thing he hears upon their turning into the lot are steel brushes upon cymbals; a stealthy, metallic sound, made more metallic, tinny, by the metal speakers from which it emanates. The sound accompanies them into the nearest aisle, the Camino prowling along in tune

25

while his father looks for an opening. The Kid looks at the screen, 3 stories-tall and long as an ice rink, watches as pink gaseous nebulae transform into Blake Edward's Pink Panther, who sits coolly on his haunches, holding a cigarette in a long, slim holder, tapping ashes. A saxophone plays Henry Mancini as his father kills the lights and noses the Camino away from the screen, begins backing into slot #29.

The kid turns around, looks across the lot as the rear of the car begins tilting upward. He's looking at the supple mounds that radiate out in a semi-circle from the screen, "like bench seating in a Greek or Roman amphitheatre," his mother once said. The mounds are smooth and solid and black. Upon them, all around, big tires crunch to a halt and brakes chirp. All around, wide hoods cant toward twilit screens like missiles.

The first movie image he sees from the back of the El Camino is from *The Legend of Boggy Creek*—a blonde boy running through a field in which everything is painted redden-gold by the setting sun, which flares off the lens and makes multicolored circles. The boy runs and runs, terrified of something behind him—something in the trees, some-thing which howls—climbing over a barbed wire fence, scrambling over stones.

THEY HIT THE SWINGS RUNNING, depositing rumps in rubber hammocks, grabbing onto chains, pumping pleated-toed sneakers in the sand. The sky swoops in and out of view as they swing, one ascending while the other falls back, and visa-versa. It is intermission.

He catches glimpses of his brother beside him, of his flushed cheeks and glittering eyes, his thick, wavy hair. He catches glimpses of the Camino, too, sees his father dusting off the lawn chairs, and digging amidst the ice chest. He doesn't see his mother but knows she is probably at the snack bar, ordering pizza or hamburgers or hotdogs in metal foil—like the heat shielding on the lunar lander— knows she'll come back smelling faintly of grease and hot-buttered popcorn and Aquanet hairspray. Still, it is odd that she has gone rather than their father, who used to use the walk as an excuse to smoke a cigarette, as if everybody didn't know exactly what he was doing.

27

He pumps his own feet in the sand, begins catching up to his brother.

"Where's Mom?"

"Dunno. She was walking toward the snack bar— there she is."

The snack bar is a blue and white rancher-style building with a flat roof of corrugated metal, which glows ghostly in the back of the lot. He scans the yellow picnic tables, sees a man in an olive-green military uniform talking to a woman with hair like a beehive, and another man with black hair and thick sideburns playing cards with two children. He sees two women smoking cigarettes—no, one is a man, a "Hippie," as his father says, like his eldest half-brother. She has already gone in, he thinks. She is somewhere behind the black glass with the muted hints of light, like distant galaxies. And there is the sun! The projector's beam—exploding from a row of small, uniform windows. The projector's beam is a white nimbus, a sun flare—an eye too potent and piercing to meet. Next to it, at another yellow picnic table, sits his mother. She is only a silhouette, but he can tell it is her because of her thickly coifed hair and the tilt of her head. He wonders what she is doing, just sitting there. She is watching them, he decides. She is smiling. Smiling at him.

He grips the cold chains of the swing, kicks harder against the sand. He *knows* she is watching. Watching as if he were a movie star on the drive-in theater screen. He waves at her gleefully. She does not wave back. He waves again—he needs her to wave back. The silhouette with the thickly coifed hair and tilted head does not wave. Why would she not wave? Maybe it is not her. Thinking about this causes him sudden terror. He looks around for his father, finds him hovering in the gloaming behind the Camino—a smudge of white and Khaki in the dark. He waves at *him*. But his father does not wave back, either. What is he doing back there? At last he says, "Think Dad is lying?"

"About what?" says his brother.

"About not smoking anymore."

"Duh. Why do you think he's always going to the snack bar?"

"He didn't tonight. Mom did."

"He will."

The Kid shrugs. He is unconvinced. "But why would he lie?"

29

"Grownups lie. So Mom won't worry. So we won't want to copycat him."

"He wouldn't lie."

Sheldon laughs and imitates their father, *"Whew,* it sure is smoky in there!"

Now they both laugh, swinging higher and higher, swinging in unison. The Kid imagines he is Spiderman, high above Manhattan, leaping from web-line to web-line. He watches his Keds—now dangling over the sand, now suspended in space—breathes it all in—his brother's company, his mother and father who are close, though not waving, the world.

THE SECOND MOVIE IMAGE he sees from the back of the El Camino, with everyone chewing and resettling and sipping from straws, is the Universal International logo, the one with a cloudless planet earth spinning slowly in outer space, which seems vaguely frightening to him. The logo is in black and white because the movie it precedes, Virgil W. Vogel's *The Mole People,* is in black and white, and is overlaid with the opening strains of the film's soundtrack, which is full of horns and drums and cymbals.

The Mole People is about a group of archeologists, one of whom is played by Hugh Beaumont, father to the Beaver, who discover a patriarchal society of albinos living beneath the earth; a society that makes human sacrifices of pretty young virgins, and employs a race of mole monsters as laborers. But what makes its mark upon the Kid is the movie's depiction of an entire underground world—a hollow earth—and how there seems to be a mysterious source of light down there, one powerful enough to illuminate everything, though what this source is they never explain. That and the mole monsters bursting from the ground—grabbing luckless victims with their big, pebbly hands, yanking them below the surface in a swirl of sand, after which, each time, Mom laughs and says, "And *awaaay* we go!"

III | Last Kid on the Moon

HE IS STANDING outside Broadway Elementary, looking for the El Camino.

His first month at school has confirmed what his mother already suspected—he has a talent for artistic expression; but there are signs he will struggle with

31

reading and with arithmetic. His teachers seem to adore him, although he gleefully disregards many of their directives, painting outside the lines whenever it suits him and inserting fanciful creatures and space vessels into what are supposed to be realistic reproductions of his life in Spokane circa 1972. He gets on well with his classmates and even shows signs of becoming 'popular,' but only after a catastrophe on the first day when, in a state of terror at his father's departure, he approached the blackboard, and—in an attempt to master his surroundings—drew a massive illustration of the *U.S.S. Enterprise,* which evoked not applause but derisive guffaws, and prompted one student, Keith, to shout, "It doesn't even exist anymore! The show's been cancelled!"

Nor does he take the bus, the size and noise of which horrifies him, but instead seeks out his father's El Camino, which stands out, stark white amongst brightly colored Volkswagens and wood-paneled station wagons, like his own colorless hair amongst his peers, and attracts the attention of everyone already aboard the bus, their faces and hands pressed against the glass.

Because the lot directly adjacent to the school is crowded with buses, the parents must park along the opposite side of the street, where they idle until openings present themselves. But when the Kid sees his mother in the passenger seat of the car—unusual since her daycare clients don't often pick up their children until shortly before dinnertime—he runs directly toward them, oblivious to the oncoming traffic. His father taps the horn once, curtly—but the Kid is already there, climbing into his mother's open door and over her lap—causing the newspapers spread there to crumple—into the center of the seat.

"How'd it go?" asks his mother.

He shrugs. "We saw a movie about kangaroos. They have a pouch, built right into their stomach."

"To carry their pups in," says his mother.

"But they can still run and jump really fast. What's that?" He points at the ball of cotton taped over her wrist.

"Mom had a boo-boo," she says.

"What kind?"

She smoothes the paper and lifts it up, covering her face completely. "Now showing, Starlight Drive-in

33

Theater: *Five Million Years...*" The engine rumbles as they pull onto the road; she does not finish the sentence.

"Mom," he says.

"We have to pick up your brother," she says, lowering the paper, and winks.

THE MOVIE SHOWING at the Starlight Theater is Hammer Films' *Five Million Years to Earth,* which begins with workers discovering the fossilized remains of prehistoric humans while digging a subway tunnel beneath the streets of London. The workers call in scientists, who promptly begin excavating the remains until they, too, make a startling discovery: There is something *else* buried down there. Something unnatural. Something constructed, and tapered, like a bomb.

The scientists call in the military, who expand the excavation until they expose the nose-cone of what they presume to be an unexploded V-2 rocket. As they continue to clear away the mud and cake, however, everyone realizes it is no such thing—that it is, in fact, something not of this earth. This proves out when they discover a handful of dead aliens in a walled-off compartment, a compartment full of hex comb, like an enormous beehive. The aliens look like huge bees, or locusts, and bleed green slime when autopsied. Imprinted upon the Kid's mind is a scene via flashback of thousands of these things marching beneath a red-brown sky—"Walking, bouncing, leaping!"—swarming across a desert waste on some apocalyptic errand of destruction.

The main character, Professor Quartermass, concludes that the object is an ancient Martian spaceship; nor is it inert, he postulates, but *alive,* and brooding over some inscrutable end. It has clearly been influencing the citizens of Hobb's End for some time, as there are newspaper accounts of sporadic outbursts of murder and mayhem going back decades. In fact, he says, it has wanted them to come and unbury it for a long time. And now that it has been unburied, it is *waking up.* Growing powerful again.

Five Million Years to Earth ends with the ship's evil influence extending throughout London, causing widespread rioting and chaos, setting the ground to trembling and to roll like water. At the climax there appears a gigantic, ghostly apparition of light, one of the bug beings magnified a thousand-fold, which looms over the city like a god. Which glares back at Quartermass, at the Kid, at his mother and father and brother, at the entire parking lot, as if from the center of time and space.

"I was here when they had that earthquake," says his father, during a shot of the ground rolling like water. "The whole car went like this..." He gestures palm down, as though his hand were a boat on the waves.

OCTOBER ROLLS INTO November, which roles into December. They continue to ride in a variety of vehicles—sometimes his dad's work truck, with its ladder racks and door signs and floor strewn with fast-food containers, other times the Ford wagon—but the Camino quickly becomes his favorite, even after it has grown too cold outside to ride in back. It becomes his favorite because it is a toy in the truest sense. There is almost nothing utilitarian about it, not even its smooth, shallow payload, which has only been used to ferry him and his brother on joyrides and for drive-in movie seating. His favorite, too, because even now, after it has grown too cold to ride outside, rather than being banished to a cool, stale, airless backseat—as in the wagon—or the crotch of the work truck, where the long gear handle constantly

36

intrudes, he and his brother can sit right between their parents—a perfect fit—and be afforded the same view. And because it is so *alive.*

There is never any doubt as to whether the Camino is running. When Dad turns the key its engine leaps up with a rumble. It is moody, too, head-down and all-business on the highway, restless and chatty on side streets, wistful on winding passes, full of hearty laughter coming back down.

When the night is long and they are in the Camino—the interior of which is incredibly spacious for a car without backseats—he dozes in the warmth of his mother's lap; or, as his mother tends to sit with her feet tucked beneath her, on the floor—with his head against the carpeted hump that contours around the transmission. If he nods off it is to the hum of the engine and the drone of the radials—steady, absolute—the blow of the heater, his mother's laughter.

Sometimes he rolls onto his back in order to watch streetlights or the tops of the power poles as they pass, but often he just watches his mother, who always seems to be gazing wistfully out the window, or chatting at his dad, or laughing heartily with her head thrown back, like

Lucille Ball. Often he imagines the engine as the street lights play over her face. Again and again the blue sparks flash, the compressed gas explodes, and the pistons drop, turning the crankshaft.

One morning while he is peeking between the door and the jamb of his parents' bedroom—looking in on his mother, who is sitting at the end of the bed, wrapping Christmas presents while cradling the telephone receiver against her shoulder—he hears her say, "I'm not going to be a prisoner to a possibility. It wasn't malignant."

The sound jumps out at him. *Malignant.* There is something course and ragged about it, like *throat.* Some of her other words have a similar affect—*lobular carcinoma—in situ—invasive breast cancer.* They make it difficult for him to concentrate on what she is wrapping—which he is convinced, by the size of the box and its coloring, is an Aurora plastic model kit: Godzilla, maybe; or King Kong, or Rodan. "It means there's an increased risk," she says. "It just needs to be watched. See? Thanks to the left we know what the right is doing." She laughs. "I'll listen, I'll listen!"

38

IT IS TWILIGHT; there is a light snow.

His father swings the El Camino into the employee parking lot of the Central Pre-Mix cement quarry on Freya Avenue, the place they stop at—after loading up on Strombolies at Mike's Burger Royal—whenever there's a moon shot. The Kid loves the quarry, loves watching the excavator carry crushed stones, like moon-rock, up from the hopper, as bulldozers and semis belch plumes of black smoke, and belts and pulleys hum and whir. His father tunes the radio while his mother hands out the Strombolies, which are wrapped in thick, white butcher-paper; tunes to a recap of what for them is the day's top story—Apollo 17. Beneath the silver winter sky, parked amidst the foothills of the towering gravel stockpiles, they listen:

"This is the CBS Evening News: Live Coverage of Apollo 17—Farewell to the Moon, with Walter Cronkite, brought to you by Tang: It's a Kick in the Glass!"

Everyone leans in, butcher-paper crumpling, marinara sauce dripping. His brother nudges him— the Camino has gotten increasingly cramped over the last several months; like the children's clothing Mother repeatedly buys only to donate a few months later.

39

"Bob, this is Gene, and I'm on the surface; and, as I take man's last step—"

A horn blasts from somewhere across the quarry, drowning the words, causing the Kid and his mother to jump.

"For God's sake," says Dad.

He turns up the volume as the horn blows and blows.

When at last it falls silent they hear Walter Cronkite say:

"And that's the way it was. Commander Gene Cernan, uttering what may be man's last statements from the Moon. Then, before the long journey back, he took a sample-return handle, and made good on his promise to Tracy, his daughter, scrawling her initials, TDC, in the lunar soil, where they will stand for all eternity."

The Kid looks down, sees his father taking his mother's hand.

"I have to pee," says the Kid.

"You always have to pee," says his brother. "Why couldn't you do that before, while we were at Mike's?"

"I didn't have to pee then," says the Kid.

"It's okay," says his mother. "Little bladders need more let." She opens her door, which makes a brief grating sound. "Just stand between me and the door, sweetie. No one will see."

"But—"

"Just do it. We've done this before. I'll keep watch."

He climbs over her and steps to the ground—a limy silt with a fresh film of snow, which compresses beneath his Keds like moon dust—and faces away. It is cold, colder than he expected after sitting in the Camino, which is warm whether the windows are up or down because of the heat flowing from under the dash. He looks at his shoes as he starts to pee, taking care not to hit them. The snow hisses and steams, as if pee is some kind of laser weapon—cutting through surface layers, burning through the earth. He gets some on his shoes after all.

The quarry workers have begun exiting the building now, hunched over lunch pails and Thermoses. He watches them as they climb into their vehicles, many of which have banged-up fenders and mismatched colors. Sheldon says something about them seeing his weenie. The Kid ignores him, hearing the motors of the workers' vehicles sputter to life, watching taillights wink on. He recognizes the Monkeys singing, *"Take the last train to*

41

Clarksville..." He pees and pees. A freight train rumbles close as the automobiles file past on his father's side of the Camino—their tires skittering between ruts, dunking in and out of potholes.

"Hi there," says his dad to each and every worker, waving politely, laughing pleasantly. "Hello—hi there...."

The Kid finishes even as the final car pulls from the lot; as the caboose of the train *clack-clacks* down the tracks.

"Remember to tap," says his mother.

"Or you'll get a pee spot," says Sheldon.

The Kid has a problem with getting pee spots, and with wetting beds. He looks at the nearby heaps of gravel—ash-gray and cold as the moon—imagines that they're part of the lunar landscape; imagines, too, that he can see the lunar-lander, crouched upon its golden, spidery legs, ready for launch.

"And with the words, 'Okay, let's get this mother out of here,' they blasted off. As television audiences on earth watched, the rover's TV camera, directed from Houston, followed their ascent until they were out of sight..."

42

He imagines a flash of light and an explosion of sparks, sees the lunar module climbing into space.

"...and then slowly scanned the now-deserted lunar surface. The awareness that no living person was around made the scene all the more impressive. It was almost possible to hear the silence."

He looks at the sky, which is a gray void, and imagines he can see stars, the Big Dipper and the Little Dipper, and the moon. He looks at the now-stilled excavator and the American flag draped over the screening tower's edge. The flag ruffles in the breeze. Now that the bulldozers have quit and the workers have gone—now that Apollo 17 has begun its final journey home—the place feels desolate. A place for winds, the souls of winds. Is this the sound of trouble? The sound of the world breathing whether people share in it or not? *That's not the sound of trouble,* says Fast Eddy, as if standing nearby. *The sound of trouble is when something goes wrong.* He looks back down at his own feet: his peeing has penetrated the silt and snow, revealing a craggy mound of wet, reddish rock, which glistens in the twilight, like the livers his mother brings home from Safeway, but soaked in pee instead of blood, which expands out from the wound, twisting, winding, splitting, spreading.

IV | Dagora-Carcinoma

"WHAT'S A 'GLOBULAR CARCINOMA?'" he asks.

His mother turns him around—roughly, it seems.

"What did you say?"

"What's—'glob—ular—carcinoma?'"

She starts to speak—laughs uncomfortably, evasively.

"Well—I...."

His parents look at each other. Nobody says anything. When she faces him again, she has made a decision. He can see it behind her eyes. "You know...I'm not really sure. Sounds like one of your sci-fi monsters. Come on, get back in. We're losing all the heat. You can have the window."

"Scoot," she tells Sheldon, and he scoots. The Kid climbs in.

"No more Apollo," says Sheldon.

44

"I guess it was inevitable," says Dad, scrunching his neck, staring up through the windshield. "We've run out of road."

The Kid stares at his own shoes.

"Hey," says his mother. She places a hand on the back of his head, smoothes his cowlicks. "Has Dad told you about the aquifer? How it constitutes an *underground* river, which runs beneath this very spot?"

"No," he says.

"Well, they've dug all the way down to it here. Next time we come by, in the daylight, sit up straight and look—over there. You may even be able to see it."

She scratches at her blouse with her free hand as she points.

He cranes and looks but sees only gravel, which no longer looks like the lunar landscape to him, and beyond that, the orange-sodium haze of downtown Spokane. But then something happens: in his mind's eye he discerns a slow-moving underground river, a river with stalactites hanging overhead and giant mushrooms crowding its banks; a river running through a subterranean world, a world of mole monsters and beautiful young virgins. A

45

river-world, presided over, perhaps, as in *The Mole People,* by some Great and Terrible Light.

It takes possession of him—the idea that something so big and so powerful, yet invisible to the eye, might in fact exist. It's what he is thinking about as his father turns the ignition and they rumble from the lot, as he steals a final look behind before the car rocks and he collides with his mother's breast, which causes her to yelp and shove him away.

"You're getting so big," she says, recovering herself.

He stares at her, numbed, then crawls into his cubby hole and lays his head on the carpeted hump. He listens to the hum of the engine and of the road, the growl of the glass packs, the blow of the heater. And though everything sounds pretty much the way it always has, he thinks he can hear the slightest difference, a vague grinding and pinging, as though something has come loose. Something beneath him—asymmetrical, divisive—something out of balance.

HE IS BEING CARRIED downstairs to bed by his father—which means he's missed the entire ride back.

46

But that's okay. He knows now that the Stock Steel building isn't where they film *Star Trek*.

His mother is with them, following behind as they reach his room near the bottom of the stairs. The room is comprised of two concrete walls and two wood-paneled ones and is a disaster zone of toys and models and stacks of comic books—one of which, because the Kid has reversed the spines every 3-4 inches, reaches half-way to the ceiling.

Because the concrete walls are only imperfectly-poured sections of foundation, his mother has allowed him to paint on them. The paintings stand in stark contrast to the rest of the room: they are uncluttered and well-organized, depicting surprisingly faithful renditions of the real world, with only the occasional intruding movie monster or starship.

"I think we're going to have someone else to do graphics," says his mother, after tucking him in. She is looking at the paintings. "In addition to Archie."

Archie is the painter they hire whenever custom work is needed—hubcaps in the style of New York's Chrysler Building for a car dealership in Coeur d'Alene, non-representational stripes and circles for a public

47

school in North Spokane, 7-foot-tall parrots for a pet store on East Sprague. His father leans against the doorframe, studying the pictures, some of which are incomplete. "Sure," he says. "These are pretty good, buddy. But you won't be able to flit from one to another on an actual job. A job must be finished, no matter what."

The Kid looks at him, then at his own paintings. "What's 'globular carcinoma'?" he asks again.

This time, his mother doesn't waver. She gestures to his father to come closer. He comes closer, puts his ear to her mouth. She whispers something, a single word; it starts with a 'T.' His father nods and leaves the room.

His mother looks at the paintings, indicates one in which a great jellyfish-like monster may be seen descending from the clouds, ganglia-like arms dangling, expanding—reaching for the city but also spreading across the sky—like lightning. "It's that," she says.

He shakes his head. "That's Dagora."

"That may be what they call him in the movie," she says. "But that's not his *scientific* name."

He stares at her, unsure whether she is having him on or not. She arches an eyebrow, like Spock. There is a squeaking sound as dad re-enters, pushing a television set atop a stand with metal wheels. The Kid recognizes the set at once; it is their old black and white RCA, the one which used to occupy the living room before they bought the big Sharp, the color one with the enormous screen and colonnaded speakers. The RCA's rabbit ears rattle against the doorframe as his father pushes it in—pushes it to the end of the Kid's bed, where the little metal wheels chirp and tweet as he rolls it back and forth, centering it, making it just so. The Kid stares blankly as his father plugs it in and pulls the chromed knob, feels the down stand on the back of his neck as the screen becomes statically charged and the hidden vacuum tubes buzz to life. A dab of light appears in the center of the glass and grows, glowing, until it fills the screen. His father rubs the top of the television and waves his hand across it, like the women on *The Price is Right*. His mother laughs.

The Kid looks from one parent to another. He looks at the wall—at Dagora—at *Dagora-Carcinoma*. "I'll have a job?" he asks.

"Someday." His mother folds and smoothes the top covers fastidiously. "But our job right now is to just be a family. Our job right now is to take a beautiful ride, in that beautiful car—to get from here to there."

His father heads upstairs, whistling. "Goodnight, buddy," he calls to Sheldon.

The Kid and his mother stare at each other. "Do I have a job right now?" he asks.

"You're job right now is to be the Kid—for as long as you possibly can." She stands and moves toward the door, pauses in the frame. "And my job is to make sure that happens." She nods at the television. "Keep it down. Use it responsibly. Or else."

She shuts off the light and eases the door partially-closed. The hallway light remains on. He lies atop his bed in the semi-dark, listening to the furnace, ignoring the TV, thinking about the underground river and the rattling sound from underneath the car, staring at the models suspended from the ceiling by fishing line, the *U.S.S. Enterprise,* the Romulan *Bird of Prey,* a Klingon Battle Cruiser, a pterodactyl. Beyond the basement window, in the dark, through the falling snow which has gotten heavier, which has begun to stick, to accumulate, he can just make out the Camino's rear bumper and tailpipe.

50

THERE IS A SCIENCE-FICTION MOVIE ON—one he doesn't warm up to initially because it doesn't have any mole monsters or underground rivers. In fact it seems rather dull and adult to him at first—not adult in the way his parents are adult, but adult in the way commercials during *The Late Show with Johnny Carson* are adult, meaning there is a lot of cigarette smoking and gambling and even, at one point, people dancing naked; though this is suggested rather than shown.

The movie is called *X: The Man with the X-ray Eyes,* and it's about a doctor who invents magic eye drops—a kind of Super Murine—which enable him to see through things: walls, clothes, skin—deeper and deeper until he sees right through to the center of creation; until he sees, in his words, "the eye…that sees us *all!"* And cannot *unsee* it.

He lays thinking about the movie long after it has ended; staring at the ceiling and his hanging models, aware the affiliate is airing *Mary Hartman, Mary Hartman*—which he hates—not paying attention to it; wondering what it would be like to have X-ray vision. Would it be like in the movie? Would it mean starting with something small, mundane, like a tiny peephole, and seeing it grow to cosmic proportions? What would happen if he, the Kid, were to actually acquire it—if *any* kid were to acquire it? Would he find the cause of the Sound of Trouble? What if it was too much for him—too strange, too beautiful, too overpowering—so overpowering it became horrible—as it did for Doctor Xavier? What if, having found it, *having looked upon the face of it,* he could not un-find it? What if he could never get his original eyes back? What if he could never go back to being just the Kid?

HE DREAMS that his bed has become the payload bay of the El Camino. The sun is setting and the color is bleeding from a copper sky, in which the Goodyear blimp floats, like a galleon, pointed in the same direction as the car, big as the *Hindenburg*. Because the sun is going down he can see the light inside the dirigible's cab, the men moving about inside. But the blimp is outpacing them—so rapidly that he must crane his neck in order to track it, which leads him to its reflection in the Camino's rear window, through which he sees an empty cab save for his mother, who is driving.

52

She cranes her own neck to look at him, smiling down, the way she did when he was a baby lying in a wash basin, being bathed by her—cool water wrung from a wet towel, dripping on his face. Her hair is thick and wavy and lush with life; her skin is tanned, her teeth white. She smiles effervescently, the last rays of the sun flaring about her. The scene shifts suddenly; it is night— now they are all in the cab: father driving, mother at the passenger window, Sheldon and himself between. The Kid stares at the back of their heads, rolling his eyes, wonders how he can be in the cab while also lying in the payload bay, alone. He watches the streetlamps over the freeway as his Camino-bed blows beneath them, imagines they are the spindly necks of Martian war machines. He counts them as they pass, 1, 2, 3, 4....

He revisits the dream many times, over many twilights, as 1972 rolls into 1973, which rolls into 1974—*bang, bang, bang,* like that.

V | World's Fair

THE FIRST COMIC BOOK he picks out for himself is an issue of *Turok, Son of Stone,* published by Gold Key

53

Comics. It captures his imagination because of its fully painted cover, which depicts a pair of Native-American warriors, Turok and Andar, doing battle with a pack of tyrannosaurs—rendered fleshy pink, like real living things. The dinosaurs remind him of the ones he has seen at drive-in theater movies like *Dinosaurus* and *The Valley of Gwangi*—realistic yet somehow *off*. His brother has told him that this is because the movie dinosaurs must be "rotor- scoped" into real-life footage—footage of square-jawed American actors in white cowboy hats and riding chaps, or blonde and buxom actresses, screaming in distress. In the book Turok and Andar have discovered a lost valley from which they cannot escape. They use poisonous arrows to combat all the dinosaurs they encounter, which they call "Honkers."

He knows this because he is slightly taller now. His hair is slightly longer, and he can read some.

He picks the book out of a rotating newsstand at the 7-11 they stop at on their way to World's Fair '74—which is being held right there, in their little city of Spokane—but feels apprehensive as he approaches his mother with it. He is afraid she might perceive in that cover, as he does, a wildness, a nakedness. He is afraid she might notice the threat of violence in the Indians' taut bows and grim expressions, or the way in which the dinosaurs' pale skin suggests moving parts just beneath the surface—strained muscles and ligaments, bones, blood.

He hands the book to her but looks outside as she flips the pages—he doesn't want her to think he wants it too badly. And he wants it badly. It is late morning and the sky is blue and cloudless. His dad is parked near the front of a line of vehicles at the gas pumps, arm cocked out the window, forehead shining. Sheldon is leaning toward him from the back, talking and gesturing. Everything shimmers in the fumy, heated air. Someone honks impatiently. The Camino lurches forward, up to the pumps. A trace of Elvis Presley singing "Suspicious Minds" creeps beneath the store's doors. So does the theme from *Shaft*.

He looks at his mom. She is scrutinizing the slim book carefully, mop of blonde hair fallen partly over her face. She rubs at the blouse beneath her left armpit as she flips the pages.

At last she hands it back, along with some nickels. He marches to the counter and plunks them down.

55

The clerk just looks at him. "Need another nickel," he says.

The Kid is confused.

The clerk taps the upper left-hand corner of the comic, where the price is printed. "They're 20 cents now."

The Kid turns toward his mother, hand outstretched, but she is already gone: She is standing in front of the store, waiting, as the Camino swings around. She is getting in. He stares, first at the Camino's polished white fenders, then his family's faces, fleshy pink, ghost-like, through the glass. The car inches forward, revving and roaring. Sheldon sticks out his tongue. Mom waves playfully.

The floor feels slightly shaky beneath him. There is a trembling in his stomach, which wants out, wants to *grow.*

"Go on, get out of here," the clerk says. He pushes the comic toward him. "It's an old one, anyway."

The boy snatches up the book and bolts out the door, but climbs between his parents rather than getting in back, so the wind will not ruffle the pages.

For the next half hour, nothing exists but the book.

On the last page he comes across an advertisement. The ad depicts a young man in dark glasses staring at his own hand—not so much a hand as an assemblage of bones. The glasses look like those worn by Dr. Xavier in *The Man with the X-ray Eyes*—the ones worn to hide the fact his eyes are mutating, becoming black pits—except these have spirals in the lenses.

The copy reads:

Greatest illusion of the century! Apparently see bones thru skin, see thru clothes, etc. Amaze and embarrass everyone!

Regular size glasses with built-in optical illusion.

X-RAY VISION SPECS…$1.85 per Pair.

He folds the page back, shows it to his mom.

"Those are just for novelty, honey," she says. "They're just regular sunglasses. They won't actually allow you to see through things."

"Oh, I know," he says.

He quickly adds: "They might help me to focus on things, though."

His mother throws back her head, laughs. "Wayne, your eyes are fine. You don't need *X-ray glasses.*"

He glances behind them, half expecting Sheldon's face pressed against the glass, mewing at him. But he can't see Sheldon's head at all, only his bellbottoms and his high-tops, crossed at the ankles.

As they accelerate onto the highway he hears the grinding and pinging from beneath the floor, only harsher, louder. His parents hear it, too.

"We better get that looked at," says his father. "Time for a check-up."

"She'll be all right," says his mom. She glances over at the odometer. "45,000 miles. Prime of her life!"

FROM THE MOMENT THEY ARRIVE, Sheldon wants to strike off for the Midway, where tens of rides and roller coasters gleam beneath the sun—including the tallest Ferris wheel the Kid has ever seen. Their mother balks, telling him he is not yet old enough to wander on his own. When they encounter Johnny and Sheila—their mother's youngest son from her first marriage, and his wife—she agrees to let Sheldon go with them to the Midway, providing Johnny stay away from the Beer Garden. The Kid shakes his head when asked if he, too, would like to go. He has not developed a taste for carnival rides like his brother. In fact he fears them. He wants to see the pavilions. He wants to see for real what he has previously seen only in books and on TV.

He carries the *Turok* comic with him throughout the fair, holding it rolled up as he roams the grounds with his mother and father. Everywhere he looks there is something to marvel at…a white building with a V-shaped roof; upon which has been painted an owl in flight, its wingspan greater than the greatest drive-in movie screen…a ski-lift, the "A & W Sky Float," which starts at a building with an angled roof and long, low profile—the Washington State Pavilion—and ends at the Iranian Pavilion, where a giant butterfly made of iron and canvas looms, perched upon its pedestal in such a way that the slightest breeze causes it to pivot back and forth (there are others throughout the park—a menagerie of Cyclopean insects—big enough, the Kid estimates, to battle King Kong).

59

The highlight becomes their visit to the United States Pavilion—a huge, teepee-like structure which is covered in white canvas and ribbed with steel cables—a structure which reminds him of Disneyland's Matterhorn but leans like the Tower of Pisa, both of which he has seen only in books and on TV. Entering its cool interior they are greeted by a curved three story-tall wall of granite, inscribed with words of the fashion he has seen during the closing credits of *Dragnet,* where a beefy, sweaty hand is seen holding a spike against a slab, while another hits it with an iron mallet, causing a sharp *gonging* sound, and leaving some kind of number, along with words to the effect of MARK LIMITED. His mother leans close. "The earth does not belong to man. Man—"

"Belongs to the earth." He stares up at her, hopeful he has gotten it right, but is not sure how to read her expression. Her eyes twinkle and she appears proud beyond words, but she appears pale, also, speechless. She gives his father a pursed little smile and heads for the box- office. He stares at the wall in awe, watched over by his father, as his mother purchases tickets for IMAX—a new form of cinema requiring a screen taller even than the wall.

That this movie will be different from any he has ever seen is made clear when, after taking their seats, his mother hands him a motion sickness bag, which she instructs him to vomit into if the flying part makes him queasy. He looks at the bag then at his mother, wondering if he should beg out, if he should feign some kind of seizure in order to escape, in order that she can lead him out by the hand and buy him a hotdog and a Coke at the Food Fair, where he can sit at a picnic table in the shade, safe, un-queasy, reading *Turok*. But then the lights dim and the screen begins to glow, and when he looks at the fabric he realizes it climbs all the way to the top of the vaulted ceiling, that it is in fact much taller than the granite wall, that it is, in fact, gargantuan.

The movie begins with a shot of the earth as seen from space, but unlike the grainy Apollo footage he has seen on the news, this earth is in color—a swirl of blue and white and tan. Beyond it lie the stars, millions of them, extending in all directions, eternally. The image is accompanied by singing, by a celestial choir which reminds him of the music in *2001: A Space Odyssey*—

61

alien, unearthly. The earth herself appears unearthly, staring down at him from all that blackness, a melancholy brooding thing, a mothering god. Then the flying begins, like an eagle through the stark blue sky, over cliffs and gorges—"The Grand Canyon," his mother whispers—while again the Kid is reminded of *2001,* of the Dawn of Man sequence, of the eerily perfect black monolith amidst the ape-people and the sunbaked badlands; of the bleached bones turned to weapons, the weapons turned to elegantly designed spacecraft.

Later in the movie the narrator says, "Smog spreads from our cities…We're trying to control smog, but the problem isn't just smog. It's waste and noise and speed and overcrowding… The problem is *us."* The Kid conjures Godzilla doing battle with the Smog Monster atop Mount Spokane before the scene shifts to an aerial view of hundreds of whining dirt bikes, cutting across the desert like buzz saws, like insect marauders, storming the steppes of Mars. But it is the following scenes that move him the most, scenes in which the camera rushes headlong through automobile traffic such as the Kid has never seen—and the movie becomes a cacophony of honking horns and wailing sirens, of screeching tires and shuffling masses of people—all of which culminates in a scene depicting a snorting, belching, garbage-eating dragon—some kind of earth mover, in fast motion— whose neck undulates like a brontosaur's, and whose block-toothed jaws scoop up mouthfuls of trash, which causes all the kids in the theater to laugh, including the Kid.

There is at least one other scene that causes him to think, but that he won't understand why until much later. It is a scene in which tens of men in orange jumpsuits and hardhats battle an oil-well blaze using hundreds of pounds of explosives, which flatten the rig when detonated, extinguishing the flames and causing an eerie silence to settle over everything. But before the roiling plumes of smoke have even cleared the screen, the fire is reborn, gushing up from the earth like a geyser. "It didn't go just like it ought to," says the foreman. "There was a little puddle of oil burning in the corner, and with that gas escaping, it just reignited."

The movie ends with Chief Seattle standing in the desert, his long, gray hair fluttering, his lined and parched- looking face bronze as the sun, into which he peers. "Thank you, sun," he says, hands held before him.

"Thank you for your light. Come again tomorrow. Have mercy on us human beings."

THEY ALL RE-GROUP, the Kid and his parents, Sheldon, Johnny and Sheila, to watch President Nixon speak. None of the adults are fond of Nixon, being Democrats of long standing, though his mother isn't entirely uncharitable, saying, "At least he ended that awful war," and suggesting he should be given credit for going to China, and sustaining the Apollo program. Nixon speaks from a podium which has been set up on a dock across the river from them, a dock which is surrounded by press boxes from the major news networks, and festooned with flags from all the nations. Dignitaries crowd the dock so that the only free space remaining is the red carpet upon which Nixon has made his entrance.

"It is a great privilege to be here on this sparkling, beautiful day," says Nixon, his forehead—which with its beetled brow and steep widow's peak reminds the Kid of Harry Osborne, AKA the Green Goblin, from the *Spiderman* comics—shining in the sun. "To speak about what this particular occasion means, not only for now and the days ahead this summer—when I hope that hundreds of thousands, and maybe millions, will come to visit, but looking down through the pages of history perhaps to the year 2000—"

The Kid sits up intently.

"...25 years from now, when we celebrate a new year that comes once in 1,000 years...."

The Kid leans forward. These are the things that get his attention. *Hundreds of thousands, maybe millions. The pages of history. The year 2000, that comes once in 1,000 years.*

"Today, we speak of the environment in terms—as we should—of cleaning up the air and water, of a legacy of parks, of all those other things that have to do with making our cities and our towns and our countryside more beautiful for our children and those that follow us. The environment means all those things, but environment also means other things to people. It means, for example, for every family in America a job so that he can enjoy the environment around him. And there are those who sometimes say that the two are in conflict..."

His mother sighs. "Here comes the political spiel," she says.

65

VI | There Might Be Klingons

WHAT SHE MEANS by this isn't clear, though her dissatisfaction is. As the President drones on the Kid loses interest—unrolling his comic and flattening it out on the grass. He stares at the cover, at Turok and Andar and the fleshy pink tyrannosaurs. He is disappointed by Nixon. By this little man in a suit across the river whose forehead reminds him of Harry Osborne and whose speech has become flat and uninteresting. He stares at Turok—leaping from a cliff, grappling the tyrannosaur's neck in his bare arms, black hair flying, his medallions jangling, the muscles of his arms rippling. He thinks of Chief Seattle, thanking the sun, speaking with such dignity and reverence, whispering almost, yet towering over everyone.

"Mr. President, will you say the magic words."

Nixon squints in the sun, mops his brow with a handkerchief. "I, at noon on this day, acting in my capacity as President of the United States, it is my high honor and privilege to declare Expo '74 officially open to all the citizens of the world."

66

And with the band playing, everything rises— dignitaries from their folding chairs, plumes of red balloons—hundreds of thousands, bleeding in and out of each other, undulating like a single living thing—confetti from cannons, gulls startled into flight. So, too, rise the hot-air balloons, colored crimson and gold, colored blue, green and white— adorned with flags and logos and hard-candy stripes; their engines firing, their circular shadows drifting lazily over the U.S. Pavilion—like planets—over the crowds, over the Kid and his mother and father and brother, over his half-brother and sister-in-law—over *everything*.

THEY ARE PLAYING *STAR TREK,* the Kid and his friends—who are also the children of his mother's daycare clients—playing in a cool expanse of basement, which consists mostly of a large, long room that his father intends to convert into a rec room, but for now remains an empty, or nearly so, concrete bunker.

"Captain to shuttlecraft *Turok,*" says the Kid, swiveling in his grandmother's old Lazy-boy, the one with the liquor stains and cigarette burns, "Do you acknowledge?" The near emptiness of the room causes his voice to echo.

Everyone looks at the forward view screen—a framed print of Bierstadt's *Looking Down Yosemite Valley.* There is no response. Naugahyde scrunches as the Kid leans forward. He rubs his chin. "This is damn peculiar..."

"Their communications systems may have been disrupted by the ionosphere," says Max. At 10, he is the oldest boy in the daycare, only a year younger than Sheldon, thus tall enough to play Mr. Spock. "It is quite strong."

The Kid swivels in his Lazy-boy, head tilting, brow furrowed. "Are you suggesting...that our view screen is malfunctioning?"

Max-Spock stands with his hands clasped behind his back, staring at Yosemite Valley. He raises an eyebrow. "It is a distinct possibility. Our sensors say the shuttlecraft is there. Our view screen says it isn't."

"Uhura—"

Uhura swivels in her chair—she is seated at a Crosley Mission Stack-O-Matic Turntable, itself stacked on cinder blocks. She has a clothespin clipped to her ear, which she adjusts, pretending to listen. "Ouch," she says. "Hailing frequencies open, sir. Still no response."

"Captain," says Sulu. The Kid swivels.

Sulu peers into his View-Master, the tall kind with the speaker in the base, which sits atop a wooden door, also laid across cinder blocks. "I'm tracking a life-form reading in the *Turok's* immediate vicinity. Whatever it is, it's closing rapidly."

"We're going down there," says the Kid.

Billy, who is nine, steps forward. "Jim, you don't know what kind of—"

"All I know is we've got a twenty-four-foot shuttlecraft down there which may or may not be in trouble, and my people are in it. Uhura, Bones, Mr. Spock…" He heads for the transporter room—a smaller, also nearly empty room adjacent to the rec room. "Mr. Sulu, you have the com."

"Yes, sir," says Sulu, whose real name is Ricky. He jumps up from his chair and hurries ahead of them, into the transporter room.

"Set us down by that shuttlecraft, Scotty," says the Kid.

"Aye, aye, sir," says Ricky.

69

The Kid marches to a filing cabinet in the corner and pulls open a drawer—begins removing phasers and communicators and a tricorder. The phasers are made out of Legos; the communicators consist of two Motorola walkie-talkies—the tricorder is a Sony portable tape recorder, which he hands to Max. They step onto the circular transporter pads, which are crudely cut out pieces of construction paper. Everyone looks at Ricky, arms at their sides.

"Energize," says the Kid.

Ricky draws forward on the throttle—a genuine throttle from a Boeing 727 given to him by his father, who is a pilot for Pan-Am—as they all begin making buzzing sounds.

THEY RUSH UP THE STAIRS, Kid-Kirk, Max-Spock, Billy-Bones, and Uhura, whose real name is Stacy. Ricky brings up the rear, having instantly become a security officer. They fall all over themselves in their haste, bouncing off each other and the walls of the staircase, giggling, making buzzing sounds. When they get to the top they pile through the kitchen frenetically, the Kid tripping over the telephone line for the second time that

70

day, for the carpet remnant that usually covers it is being washed. He steadies himself against the door jamb as the others file past, then bolts after them, banging out the screen door and running through the breezeway, dashing to the center of the back yard where they retake their positions, everyone still going, *"Bzzzzzz...."*

It is May. The sky is a blue dome in which not a single cloud can be seen. There is a slight breeze, which ruffles the Maple leaves—some of which have yet to bud. The Kid scans the yard, face and arms warm, already shiny with the first sweat of summer. The El Camino waits patiently, parked beside the clothesline in the shade of an enormous weeping willow which dominates the back yard, its canopy of vines acting as an umbrella, gnarled roots visible in the grass, like the partially submerged tentacles of an octopus.

"There she is," says the Kid, pointing at the Camino. "Ensign Ricky, you take the flank. Spock, Bones, Uhura, follow me."

They all move out, Ricky going around the weeping willow while the others head straight for the Camino. "Phasers on stun," says the Kid, approaching the clothesline, which is bowed beneath the weight of drying

71

clothes; of socks and pants and shirts and towels, of sun-lit sheets like milky gauze, billowing like sails, edges flapping. The carpet remnant from the kitchen is still quite wet, dripping into the grass. They pause amongst the sheets, huddling close, Lego phasers poised beneath chins. The Kid and Max-Spock peer between the fabrics, examining the Camino-shuttlecraft, white butterflies fluttering past.

"Everyone on guard," says the Kid. "There might be Klingons."

"There's the ship," says Billy-Bones. *"Ain't she a beaut!"*

"You mean the shuttle," says the Kid—crossly. He doesn't like his narrative being interrupted.

"I mean the *ship,* the *Enterprise,"* says Billy-Bones. "For real, up in the sky."

The Kid follows Billy's gaze to where a jet airplane is cutting across the sky, a tiny white cross against all that blue, wing lights blinking, fuselage gleaming, leaving a contrail through the atmosphere like a wake in water, or a wound in flesh. Something tickles his arm and he looks down to find a tiny spider scrabbling along his skin. He shakes it off, the tip falling from his phaser. He is reaching for it when Ricky cries out from the far side of the weeping willow. They all look toward the sound, see grasshoppers scattering as Ricky's red shirt dances erratically amongst the weeds.

"Owe! Owe!" hollers Ricky. "Help! *Owe!*"

The Kid looks at Max-Spock, who raises an eyebrow.

They enter into the field, waving phasers, tramping down weeds. But when they reach Ricky they realize he isn't playing; he is being swarmed by bees—yellow jackets—the insects whirring about him like a cloud, crawling over his belly, flitting about his hair. "Owe! Owe!" cries Ricky, falling into the weeds, rolling over and over. "I'm allergic! I'm allergic!"

The Kid feels an acidic, burning poke on his arm and swats a yellow jacket away; the burning intensifies as yet another yellow jacket stings him on the cheek. Everyone starts screaming, especially poor Stacy, whose bare legs are crawling with bees.

The Kid runs away, dropping his phaser, batting at his arms. He runs faster than he has ever run before, not looking back, hearing Stacy—hearing everyone—screaming. He runs beneath the clothesline and down the

73

corridor of fabric, like the Star Gate in *2001,* slapping the sheets aside, the avenue in front of the house whooshing and humming, the bees seeming to buzz in his ears. He runs until he collides with the screen door and tears it open, until he collides with his mother, who has heard the commotion—who, when he tells her about the swarm, goes immediately to the phone and dials 9-1-1, but then taps the hang-up button again and again—listening, tapping, listening, tapping.

The Kid looks at the floor, at the gray telephone line, kinked and lying loosely.

"Round up everyone in the house," says his mother. "I'll meet you in the Camino, out front."

The Kid doesn't say anything, only stares up at her, his right cheek burning and swelling. "Ricky's—"

"Allergic to bee stings, I know." She snatches the keys from the wall. "Hurry."

VII | Shifting Gears

IT IS AMAZING TO HIM, unbelievable, how his mother manages the situation. In the space of five minutes she is able to rescue everyone from the swarm, to get poor Ricky, who is bloated up like a movie corpse and visibly yellow, who could possibly be dying, into the cab of the car, along with Max and himself, to watch over him, and to get them on the road, flying up Mission Avenue to Valley General Hospital, flying so fast the Kid presses against the seat and sticks his foot against the dash, feeling small, cowardly, the Camino's payload full of kids, its engine roaring, her own arms covered in swollen welts, her temper calm except when a truck full of gravel swings into the lane right in front of them, startling him, making him flinch and cover up, creating a knot of terror in his stomach, but also slowing them down, causing rocks to hit the windshield, leaving bitter little divots in the glass.

"Well," she says, as they rumble up to the Emergency Room entrance, *"That'll* spread."

RICKY SURVIVES, but they do not play *Star Trek* again for the rest of Memorial Day Weekend, nor the Memorial Day Weekend after that. In fact they do not play it again, or if they do, the Kid is not aware of it. Something has changed; he has been rattled by his failure with the bees, by his lack of courage, his abandonment of his friends. Kirk would never have done that, abandoned his post. Neither would Sheldon, who is tough, athletic, no-nonsense—who is more like Kirk than he will ever be, who even looks like him. The Kid does not ever want to play Kirk again. Instead he plays *Kolchak.* It is June.

Carl Kolchak is the lead character of ABC's *Kolchak: The Night Stalker*—a fast-talking, funny-walking reporter for the "Independent News Service" (which, though he is not quite nine, even the Kid knows is only a movie set— there's a logo at the end of every episode which reads, 'Filmed at Universal Studios in Hollywood, California'). Unlike the world of *Star Trek,* however, Kolchak's world looks and sounds just like the Kid's, only it is filled with every manner of supernatural intrusion, from a vengeful, headless motorcyclist to a bayou swamp monster in Chicago.

The biggest difference is that he plays Kolchak *alone,* in the twilight hours before dusk, after the children of his mother's clients have all gone home. Not even Tony Vincenzo, Kolchak's brash but lovable editor, warrants casting. The Kid plays all the parts himself, even the women, who are always begging him not to go out—tugging on his imaginary tie, taking off his straw hat (which he has found amongst the moldy treasure of dead relatives beneath the stairs), telling him that the story can wait, it's dangerous, that there's monsters out there but only them in here, that he should come back to the bedroom and make love to them, whatever that means.

Like Kolchak, he begins carrying a portable tape recorder, formerly Max-Spock's tricorder, everywhere—recording television programs, bits of conversation, radio newscasts. The newscasts are of special interest to him—Bobby Fischer surrendering the World Chess Championship to Anatoly Karpov, the Lebanese civil war, the Fall of Saigon—as he has begun to think of himself as a reporter, or at least a reporter-in-training. Occasionally he even tries to make secret recordings, like former President Nixon, recordings of his parents discussing payroll and business decisions; or Sheldon and his older friends discussing sex and how it might work. But all he ever gets is gray noise—an indistinct *whooshing*—from which few words can be extracted.

One day when he is doing this, standing on tip-toe behind the cinderblock fence in the back yard, by the brick barbecue pit, holding the tape recorder high above

77

his head, recording Sheldon and his friends talking, his father says out of nowhere, "Hey little buddy, how about a drive-in movie?"

The Kid panics, if only for an instant. Not because his father will lecture him about the moral failing of recording private conversations—one should be so lucky, he doesn't pay that much attention—but because Sheldon will realize he's been there all along. This too proves unfounded when Sheldon, overhearing, hollers, "It's my turn to pick the movie!"

But they do look at him funny, Sheldon and his friends, when they come through the gate. The Kid is holding his tape recorder and wearing his straw hat, the band of which holds an index card—PRESS, in Magic Marker. Everyone stares at him as though he were some kind of museum exhibit, even his father. Nobody says anything. The whole scene has caught the Kid off guard. Sheldon seems so much taller all of a sudden, he and his friends.

A yellow jacket buzzes past, insidious little legs dangling. The bees have gone and come again. So has drive-in movie season.

Bang, bang, bang, like that.

78

TO GET TO THE STARLIGHT they must first pass the Y Drive-in Theater, called so because it is located at the far northern end of Division, where the avenue splits into two separate highways, US 395 north and US 2 northeast, which leads to the Starlight. A chain of vehicles extends from beyond the theater's marquee—which is topped by an enormous yellow 'Y,' in outline only, so that one can see right through it. The procession is such that it spills out onto Division Avenue, forcing his father to change lanes.

The Kid peers into the idling vehicles as they swoosh past, sees men and women of all ages, some by themselves but many more in couples. There are few if any families—none he can recognize as being like his own, with a mother and a father and some siblings. In fact there are no children at all. He looks at the marquee, recognizes one word instantly but has to struggle with the other. His brother notices him struggling and says, "Deep Throat."

He must look confused.

"That's what's playing," his brother says.

79

The Kid frowns. The words sound menacing to him—black, guttural. He stares at the theater's sheet metal walls and the ghostly green glow beyond—at the endless chain of vehicles inching forward beneath the marquee. Their passengers seem more than mere moviegoers to him, but keepers of some solemn secret.

"What's it about?" he asks.

His brother laughs, good naturedly, insincerely. "Ask Mom," he says.

The Kid looks at him, uncertain. He cranes his neck around the Camino's cabin, the night-wind blasting his hair back, intending to do just that, to ask their mother— is surprised to find her window rolled up. She does not even notice him but remains intent on her conversation with his father, who doesn't notice him either, though he is looking directly at him, or so it seems. He knocks on the glass. His mother turns her face to him, putting on a smile, but looks away before he can indicate that she should roll down her window.

He slumps against the wheel-well, watching his parents through the rear window, wishing he could read their lips—the way HAL read Bowman and Poole's lips in *2001*—wondering what it could be his parents are talking about; what secret Sheldon is keeping from him, what secrets they themselves keep from him and his brother, and noticing, too, that his mother is no longer smiling; that her broad grin just moments before was for his benefit, and his alone.

THERE IS NO WAITING to get in at the Starlight, possibly because it is already dark and the movie has started, or at least the ads and cartoons. The Kid records everything— the rumble of the Camino's engine, the crunching of pebbles beneath the tires, the ratcheting of the emergency break. He is in the process of recording the opening theme to *The Pink Panther* when his brother snatches the hat off his head and vaults over the quarter panel, hollering, "A good reporter never loses his hat!"

The Kid leaves the recorder where it lays, on the roof of the Camino, just above his mother's head, leaping after Sheldon, his Keds slapping the concrete too hard, causing his feet to sting. He sprints toward his brother— who sprints toward the playground beneath the screen— running up and down over the great undulating concrete humps, pounding past other kids and their families, darting between parked cars. He leaps over the railroad

81

ties and splashes across the sand, tries to snatch the hat off Sheldon's head, but his brother swings too fast, swooping up and down in great pendulous arcs, laughing. The Kid is not sure how to respond—is his brother laughing with him or at him? Should he laugh right back or should he be angry? He decides to laugh right back. He decides it is a game they are playing. That it should be fun.

"I piss in that hat," he says, giving up. He goes to the nearest swing, grabs the chains in mock anger. He kicks off, quickly gaining momentum, squeezing his feet together to form a knife while ascending, folding them under his seat when descending. He cranes his neck to see the screen, sees the Pink Panther wavering between the tops of animated buildings. Panther is trying to cross a traffic-choked boulevard by nailing one plank after the other, but it isn't working. The bonds keep loosening and the planks keep sagging, sending him scrambling back to the beginning, re-nailing the anchor. The cartoon reminds him of another he has seen on TV, in which Wiley Coyote runs off the edge of a cliff—but hangs suspended in mid- air until the instant he looks down, which sends him plummeting.

82

He looks over at Sheldon, who is wearing his hat with the brim angled toward his nose, like a gangster. Their mother has allowed him to grow his hair out like the rest of the boys; it flows from beneath his hat like Chief Seattle's, though not nearly so long, dishwater blonde instead of gray. Every few cycles his brother runs a few steps along the ground, causing sand to fishtail behind his heels. The Kid watches him, swinging, laughing, proud of whom his brother has become, is becoming—but sees they have lost their timing. While before they were synchronized now they are not. Now Sheldon ascends while he falls back, and even when Sheldon descends, he, the Kid, seems always to be falling behind. It amazes and frightens him how fast Sheldon can go, how high, so high it seems only two things are possible, that he will tumble backward from his swing and die upon the sand, or continue full circle, as though orbiting earth herself.

Either way he knows that he will never keep pace, will never catch up nor even keep sight of him. He stops trying, preferring to swing casually, leisurely. He doesn't really understand it, the more he thinks about it, this need to go fast, this love of velocity for velocity's sake. He

83

suspects his own love of car riding is very different from his brother's. It would never have occurred to him, for example, to rev the Camino's engine. To what end? For the satisfaction of hearing its roar? The excitement of making its pistons pump faster? There is something wrong with that idea. Something wasteful.

On their way back to the car Sheldon takes the hat off and sets it back on his head. "You know I love you, Bro," he says. He punches his arm softly. "Ya little shit."

"That's because you're gay," says the Kid, and punches him back, in the arm—hard as he can—bolting toward the car.

HE IS BORED TO DEATH by Sheldon's movie choices, a western and a Civil War picture. They are too realistic and mundane. What is the point of making movies, he wonders, if not to show something one cannot see in real life? The movies are all 'he said, she said,' talking and gunfire, pointless action. There are no black monoliths, no ape-men becoming space-men, no monsters, no mystery, only surfaces. The Civil War movie is the worst, lacking even interesting scenery, only ragged men marching forever across a gray and barren waste,

84

marching and marching and marching; he falls asleep only to wake and find them still marching. There is one soldier in particular, hobbled by a leg wound, his head in bloodied rags, teeth mostly missing, who reminds him of Fast Eddy but says the crudest things; who taunts the other soldiers even though they are only trying to help him.

"I wish that guy would hurry up and die," he says— only to be reprimanded by his mother, who tells him she never wants to hear that again, even in jest.

He is taken aback by her response, by its coldness and finality; by the implication he should be judged upon something he has said just to say something, to be cute, to be the Kid. Is that not his job? Is that not that what she'd said—that his job was to be the Kid, for as long as possible, and that her job was to make sure that happened? Has something changed?

He spends the remainder of the movie alone, lying in his sleeping bag atop the El Camino, watching satellites float past, fancying they are UFOs, until a front rolls in, blotting the stars, and heat-lightning begins flashing, silently, fast as an eye-blink, from cloud to cloud.

85

VIII | The Wasps in the Window Well

KOLCHAK DOES NOT QUIT. He digs, gets to the bottom of things.

It is late. He is watching a rerun of *The Night Stalker* on ABC, on his black and white TV in his bedroom. The episode is titled "The Sentry." He is excited because the summary in *TV Guide* suggests that Kolchak encounters some kind of small tyrannosaur in an underground storage facility—a small tyrannosaur, for the Kid, meaning *allosaur,* no question. The show begins as usual with Kolchak entering an empty, darkened newsroom, whistling like the Kid's father, tossing his hat onto the coat stand (which he always misses), and seating himself at a typewriter where he bangs out: DARREN MCGAVIN AS—then the title of the program. Then the clock and fan stop and he looks over his shoulder and the frame freezes, fading out on his terrified eye.

"The Sentry" begins with Kolchak in a Merrymount Archive, Inc. golf cart, humming down seemingly endless corridors lit with banks of white florescent lights, until he stumbles upon a labyrinth of rough-hewn tunnels, lit only by propane torches. "This is one story I

86

may not get to file in person," he says into his tape recorder, "so I'll have to talk fast." This is followed by flashbacks in which two Merrymount employees, Kipper and Coogan—who is last seen installing light bulb fixtures in a seemingly endless corridor—are killed. The men are killed by a clawed, scaly thing in the dark—heard but barely seen—which smashes lights one after the other as it approaches. "And now," says Kolchak, *"it's after me."*

But Kolchak is always one step ahead. When he wants to see the autopsy of a victim he dresses in scrubs and goes right in; when he wants to examine the locations of the killings he poses as a representative for a company seeking to rent storage space; when told by the General Sales Manager—Ritchie Cunningham's father from *Happy Days*—that there's no time to view the facilities today, Kolchak just smiles and escorts him into the elevator. When the G.M. has a confrontation with an eccentric staff scientist, Dr. Verhyden, Kolchak listens, eyes darting back and forth between them, while Verhyden speaks of "mysterious occurrences" and "strange people who aren't what they appear to be." When the G.M. has to take a phone call from Irene

Lamont, a comely, leggy Police Lieutenant with a history of spellbinding and misdirecting reporters (all, that is, except Kolchak), Kolchak does what any good reporter would do, he ducks from the room—into the Union Workers' break room, where he chats up a worker eating lunch, works him for info, telling him he's an insurance investigator, bribing him with everything in his wallet, asking him where was Kipper's body found? Was Coogan killed in Sector R? His body was found in Sector M? Where's Sector M? No, no, they haven't changed the alphabet, ha-ha! Then M comes before R, Sector M is on the way to Sector R, ha-ha, sure… How do I get out to see M and R? Just follow the signs, sure. I'm a fool to go out there without extra hazard pay? Ha-ha!

The Kid is startled when the commercials come on—the audio level is so much higher than the program's. He cranks the volume down, glancing at the ceiling tiles, directly over which lays his parents' bedroom. The near-silence is startling in its own right. He hears something tick against the window high on the wall, so softly he wonders if he has imagined it. Then it comes again, barely audible, *tick…tick,* as though the slightest twig is brushing the glass. On the TV, Kolchak searches dark halls with a big silver flashlight—swishing its beam back and forth over the ceiling, illuminating broken bulbs in pools of light.

THE STEP LADDER RATTLES as he sets it sideways beneath the window, pressing the aluminum hinges down, locking its legs. "I'm gonna rip the lid off this lizard creature affair," says Kolchak on the TV. "And I'm gonna find out who those guys in the water department *really* are..." The Kid climbs the ladder slowly, gripping his flashlight. He can hear the ticking clearly now that he's closer to the glass. "Carl, look..." —Tony Vincenzo again, Kolchak's brash but lovable editor—"Just drop the whole thing. I told Lt. Lamont that I would agree to back-peddle to keep you from hindering her investigation. She agreed if anything happened to phone the exclusive directly to me."

The Kid pauses on the third rung from the top, his legs trembling—he is not quite eye-level with the window. It will have to do; he doesn't want to go higher. He hears a door jamb squeak down the hall—his brother, he supposes, making a bathroom run.

"To you?" says Kolchak. "To me."

89

"Not to me?"

"No."

"To you?"

"Yes."

He switches on the flashlight. The first thing he sees before the beam dims is a solitary yellow-jacket—scurrying along the molding on the other side of the glass. It startles him—in the brief white flare—the angry yellow stripes, the busy little legs, the undulating thorax.

"You sucker. Because she ain't *never gonna call,* and I think that it comes from *very high up."*

He bangs the flashlight against his palm, trying to revive it. It pulses white and burnt-ocher. He aims it through the window, pressing its lens against the glass. Two more wasps scurry past, then a third, a fourth, some in the opposite direction so that they pile and flop over each other. The flashlight's beam falters. He bangs it against his palm, sees the papery edge of a hive before the brown beam dims to nothing. He is shaking with excitement, can barely hold the flashlight; his legs feel like rubber. He climbs back down the ladder.

He empties the dead batteries onto his bed, finds his tape recorder, uses a penny to open the little hatch. He pries out the batteries—smooth, shiny polyethylene coatings reassuring his fingertips—loads them into the flashlight, *thwump, thwump,* like missiles in a grenade launcher. He glances at the TV, where Kolchak is climbing into a wooden crate marked: FRAGILE / PRECISION INSTRUMENTS. "Watch the hat!" says Kolchak as they tamp the lid down. "You are now a precision instrument," says one of the tampers.

He remounts the ladder, ascending more confidently, pausing nonetheless on the third rung from the top. He aims the flashlight carefully, wanting, when he thumbs it on, to see it all in a rush; the hive in its entirety, the scurrying bees, the crepe paper layers. He slides the magnet-switch forward. Nothing happens. He slides it back and forward, still nothing. He unscrews the base of the flashlight. The batteries slide into his palm—clicking, rolling—he fumbles them in his excitement, holding onto one while the other claps and clangs down the rungs of the ladder.

He grips the aluminum legs, doesn't breathe.

"Carl," says Lt. Lamont on the TV, "if you have any info that will shed light on this you better start belching it up, or I guarantee you a graduate degree in license plate making down at the state farm. You don't know how bad I can be."

"Oh, I got a pretty good idea, baby!"

He climbs down gingerly and gets under the covers, switching his pillow to the foot of the bed so he can watch the rest of the show. He still is not convinced that his mother has not heard, that she is not cinching her bathrobe and heading his way right now. He watches *Kolchak,* knowing she could not punish him for watching his favorite show, on the TV *they* put in his room. Kolchak is being spoken to by the Union Foreman/U.S. Colonel, one of Verhyden's "strange people who aren't what they appear to be," saying, "Look, I don't know how long I can hold off Miss Lamont. She wants to bust you bad. Open up with me."

The Kid exhales, rolls onto his back. He stares at the ceiling tiles.

"Yeah, well, it's little things, like how you've kept a lid on all this. Yeah, see, you think that maybe there's more of these creatures. That maybe they'll get into your secret silos, your underground missiles and SAC bases— maybe they have already, huh? Well—did you ever think they might be down there in the subways too and underground tunnels and underground garages? Did ya ever think about that? I mean, when you gonna warn the general public about this?"

"When we feel the time is right."

"And *who* is *we?*"

Then there's a crashing sound and the kid flips around, sees the titular creature, "The Sentry," crashing through the cinderblock wall. But it is not an allosaurus. It is just a crocodile-like thing which walks like a man and is the size of a man, with arms like a man, and legs like a man. When the commercial break comes there is dead silence, followed by a title card which reads: STAY TUNED FOR THE CONCLUSION OF "THE SENTRY." TUNE IN NEXT WEEK FOR HEE-HAW. KOLCHAK: THE NIGHT STALKER HAS BEEN CANCELLED BY ABC. The last thing he hears before falling asleep is a worker yelling, "Verhyden's dead, and I'm getting' out of here. You're on your own!"

HE DREAMS that he is at the Starlight Drive-in Theater, swinging next to Sheldon, who knifes his legs and arches his back, swinging higher and faster with each pendulous arc. In the dream he has forgotten their differences. He has forgotten that he himself would prefer to swing slowly, leisurely, and so kicks the sand again and again, trying to catch up, trying to fly as high as his brother. But he cannot do it; he feels mired in the air like quicksand, his limbs made of concrete, while Sheldon swings faster and higher, laughing, his velocity making a whooshing and whirring, like radial tires on the highway or yellow jackets swarming, or the sound of dead air in secret tape recordings. Surely Sheldon must know something that he does not. Sheldon has been given a secret gift or curse as it may be; whatever, it has made him taller, smarter, more powerful. He flies while the Kid, who has come to a complete stop, can only watch: as his brother swings higher and higher, becoming harder and harder to track, until he cannot see him at all, only blackness, the straw hat fluttering down, the empty swing swaying, chains jangling, its rubber seat rocking from the sudden imbalance.

IX | Catalyst

AS JUNE ROLLS INTO JULY, Sheldon rides with the family less and less, preferring to play ball with his Little

League or sleep at his friends' houses. The Kid, too, becomes bored with just "riding." By now it is the *same old* scenery blowing past, the *same old* night-world. He lies in the vibrating bed of the Camino and gazes up at the high-tension towers along Upriver Drive—imagining Godzilla stalking through the darkness, keeping pace. When they pass the fuel farms by Hillyard—which remind him of industrial Tokyo from the Toho monster films—there's Godzilla again: wading through the buildings, destroying silos with his blue-white-hot radioactive breath (which sets his tree-like dorsal fins aglow). The Kid finds he can make anything in Spokane interesting by imagination alone. Gradually he forgets about Dagora-Carcinoma and the beehive inside his window well. Gradually he forgets about wanting to know what others won't tell him, about penetrating surfaces. Over-laying the world with fantasy seems good enough.

This continues until he comes across a picture in *Famous Monsters of Filmland Magazine* which is not the usual touched-up still but a genuine behind-the- scenes snapshot. The picture depicts a technician dressed as Godzilla from the waist down, ruggedly-textured legs—

keg-like in their enormity—held in place by thick suspenders (the image reminds him of the before-and-after weight-loss ads he has seen in his mother's magazines, usually a grinning, waif-thin Sandy Duncan posing in a single leg of the pants she'd worn "before"); while the top of the suit sits upon a nearby workbench, wires trailing, so that you can see right into it. You can see foam latex ganglia and glandular, sweat-soaked padding, bands of cables and tubing, gaffing tape, staples.

The technician meanwhile is a middle-aged Japanese male, balding and over-weight, who is sweating beneath the hot lights and appears wiped-out.

He is having himself a cigar.

From that point on, whenever he sees the Big G, he sees *through* the suit. He sees the foam latex ganglia and the glandular, sweat-soaked padding. He sees the balding fat man with his cigar, itself burned down to the stub.

THEY ARE HUDDLED in a booth at a Chinese restaurant when he asks his mother why comic books cost 25 cents now rather than 20, or 15. He is nine going on ten. The leaves on the trees are green. He is a little taller and his hair is a little longer.

She tells him it is because of inflation, and that it is a good example of how important it is to have an understanding of mathematics, which he has been struggling with in school. She has a keen grasp of mathematics, he knows, though she calls them "economics." She keeps the books for his father's painting company as well as her own daycare business, keeping everything humming along, often talking of "robbing Peter to pay Paul."

"I know you hate it, honey," she says, "but it's something you'll have to grow into. The dinosaurs couldn't adapt and that's why they became extinct."

This is his mother's version of *You'll shoot your eye out,* tailored just for him.

He reads his magazine as she talks, a special issue of *FM* dedicated exclusively to the films of Ray Harryhausen. He is reading about the scene in *One Million Years B.C.* where Raquel Welch is snatched up by a pterodactyl and flapped, kicking and screaming, to its nest among the cliffs. The effect was achieved by manipulating foam-latex puppets with steel armatures

97

inside one frame at a time, then matting the action together. He looks up from a picture of a giant crab (from Harryhausen's *Mysterious Island*) and notes the broken shells on his plate, figures he can stick coat hangers in them and animate them, as Harryhausen did—if his parents ever buy him a movie camera.

"…you can't be an astronaut if you don't know your times tables," his mother is saying.

"Or a graphics painter," says his dad.

"Like Archie," says his mother.

"I don't want to be an astronaut *or* a graphics painter," he says.

Nobody says anything for a while. Not even about The Bankruptcy, which has come up a lot lately when things get this quiet. Things have gotten this quiet a lot.

"We can't afford a movie camera right now," says his mom.

Everybody eats in silence.

When the smiling waitress delivers the bill on a little tray with three fortune cookies, his mom rummages through her purse and withdraws her checkbook. It isn't until after she's laid the check in the tray and returned the book that he notices an oblong black box where the

98

checkbook had been. She pushes it toward him with a pale finger, glancing at his dad who doesn't respond but seems as taken aback as the Kid. At the top of the box is stenciled: JOHNSON SMITH TOY & NOVELTY COMPANY.

He stares at it and then at her.

"Go ahead," she says.

He opens the box.

The X-Ray glasses are there. He knows they are X-Ray glasses because the words X-RAY VISION have been printed in white bloc letters across their top. They are wafer-thin, as though made of paper. They *are* paper—but thick paper. Their rims glint darkly, flickeringly, by the table's little candle. The glints are printed on the paper. The "lenses" are red and white paper spirals, but at the center of each lays a pupil of translucent film—the real lenses—which catch the candlelight and refract purple-orange.

His mom pushes the lid down, gently.

"Math first, when we get home. I'll help you."

His mind is swimming.

"Okay," he says.

"You can have them after summer school, when we pick you up."

"Okay."

"We love you, son."

"Okay."

"Even if you don't want to be a graphics painter," says his dad.

"Like Archie," says his mom. "Or an astronaut."

He lowers his head. He ducks beneath the table and comes up wearing his werewolf mask—a cheap, plastic, black and green one he's had since Halloween—which he wears slung over his back, like a sombrero. He's put cored-out crab legs on his fingers.

"I *vawnt* to suck your blood," he says, pretending to bite his mother's neck.

"That's Dracula!" she protests.

He crawls under the table and comes up on his dad's side, attacking him. He shakes his claws at the elderly couple in the booth next to them, growling. He leaps into the aisle and howls at the wait staff, all of whom cover their faces, feigning terror. Everyone laughs. Especially his mother, who does so with her head thrown back and her fingertips touching her long-sleeved blouse, just beneath her armpit, as though needing to hold something in place.

WHEN THEY PICK HIM UP from summer school the next day, he notices the black box, like a little coffin, sitting on the dash right away. It would make a neat shot in a movie, he thinks, that black box, just the way he sees it, from the bed of the Camino, through the rear window, with the reflections of treetops sliding past. His mother looks at him over her shoulder as if to say, well? That would make a neat shot too, the treetops flowing up her face like that, like water. He turns away, slumps against the cab, so that he and his mother are essentially sitting back to back. He whips the math test from his peach-colored folder and holds it over the bed rail, letting it rattle and snap in the wind. She snatches it from him and rolls up her window. He grins. The Camino's engine rumbles along.

Moments later he hears music again—looks sidelong to see his mother reaching around the cab, handing him the case. At first he pretends not to see her, but then snatches the box from her grip. He opens it immediately and takes out the glasses, unfolds the frames. Printed

101

inside are instructions: HOLD YOUR HAND TOWARDS THE LIGHT SPREAD FINGERS AND SEE THE BONES. He slides them on, hooking the cardboard frames around his ears, and then holds his hand up to the sun, spreading his fingers.

The effect, such as it is, is interesting. The lenses create a kind of aura around his hand and each finger, causing their edges to glow orange and purple. The result is that his fingers themselves become the bones, the creases in their flesh mimicking the creases between joints. He finds that the further he moves his hand away, the more intense becomes the effect; when held at the greatest distance, it really does appear as though he can see through his fingers, the halos having grown so much that the silhouettes of his fingers shrink, becoming more bone-like. He looks at the neighborhood flashing by but sees no appreciable effect, other than a slight glow about the treetops and the power poles, the rooftops, the crisscrossing power lines.

WHAT HE HAS TOLD NO ONE is that he has fallen further behind in school than anyone could guess, not just math. That his passing of the test is a freak accident, a fraud—a combination of his mother's help and the teacher's choice of questions and his ability to look cross-eyed at his classmate's papers. What he has told no one, what does not show up on his report cards, is that he spends the bulk of each class drawing pictures in his binder, pictures of King Kong and Godzilla and Rodan and King Ghidora. That when he is not drawing he is writing, but not what he has been instructed to. Instead he writes about sea serpents and UFOs and the saber-toothed cat, Sagra—his own creation, whom he pits against the others—who is undefeated except for Kong, who always wins, who was his brother's monster, before his brother forgot him, abandoned him.

103

Part Two

I | Drag Race

HE HAS BEGUN TO NOTICE a pattern to all their riding about Spokane.

His parents revisit the same places over and over— his Uncle Shane's painting business, for example, which is huge in comparison to his father's, and which looks like an auto dealership with its neon signs and fleet of trucks, and his grandfather's painting business, housed in an enormous brick building in Hillyard, a building with the words SPITZER INC. painted across the top, each letter the height of a man. They also visit a nightclub called the Pine Shed, where his uncle's white Lincoln-Continental is often spotted, as well as a little house in Platter's Ferry, where his mother's first husband and young wife are said to live. Yet they do not visit these places so much as orbit them, slinking around their peripheries like spies, the Camino's engine purring and growling.

107

East Trent Avenue is the common corridor between everything, a wide, long stretch of road which cuts through but also connects most of Spokane's industrial zones. There are Quonset huts all along this strip, which, again, like the fuel farms near Hillyard, the Kid likens to the miniature sets in Japanese giant monster movies. He is especially fascinated by the U.S. Army Reserve depot at Spokane Industrial Park, just off the far eastern end of the avenue, where he often spots military vehicles, nothing so grand as a tank or artillery piece, but at least a few camouflaged jeeps and sometimes an armored personnel carrier, slumbering in the stockade beneath the cool dark of the elm trees, like animals in a zoo. The thing about Trent Avenue for him is that it runs parallel to all the most familiar sights, like the Disneyland Railroad past the Primeval World—which he has not actually experienced but has seen on *The Wonderful World of Disney*. It covers the entire distance from downtown Spokane to Grandpa Spitzer's house in Otis Orchards—a clean, quaint affair until you go into the basement, which is missing an entire wall so you encountered a dark, moist face of dirt, root and rock.

They are idling at a stoplight on Trent—the Kid sitting in the bed of the Camino with his back to the cab—when a black Pontiac Firebird pulls alongside and begins revving its engine. The car is full of teenagers, one of whom leans out the backseat window and asks the Kid if he gives blowjobs.

"Because you sure got a pretty mouth," says the young man, who is wearing a crimson and gold letterman's jacket, and looks to be about sixteen. His eyes and hair are dark, stupid, like an animal's. His head seems wide as a watermelon.

The Kid doesn't say anything, partly because he is in his own universe, partly because he has no idea what blowjobs are, has never even heard of them. But the intent of the comments is clear. He knows that if Sheldon were here he might vault over the bed rail and smash the guy in the face—but Sheldon isn't here. For all the Kid knows, Sheldon is with *them,* the teenagers. Sheldon even *looks* like this guy, at least when he's mad—minus the dark eyes and watermelon head—has the same iron gaze, the same unexamined confidence—it is an older brother thing, he suspects. There is a girl in the car as well, who puts her thin face next to the guy's

109

and coos, *"Oooh,* I'll bet you he does. Look at all that pretty blonde hair." She has long, blonde hair herself, which curls away from her face as though blown by the wind, and is wearing too much blue eye-shadow.

His mother laughs bitterly. "I doubt you even know what you're saying, young lady."

All the teenagers laugh, as though his mother were the funniest thing on earth. Something about this angers the Kid more than he can account for. The girl is the worst of all—piggybacking off the guy, piggybacking his power, the power of the car—laughing at his mother like that, who is so much her superior; not because she is a grownup but because she makes her own power, and would never have clung to a boy like *that,* a gorilla, a bulldog, *a pig.* He feels a compulsion to dominate the girl, to degrade her. It is not just because she is degrading him. There is something about her—the long face, the long eyes, the soft pale skin, pressed against the boy's—something repellent and alluring. Something which challenges him. Something hostile and yet promising, if he can tame it.

110

He fumbles for his X-Ray glasses and slides them on, looks the girl up and down. "I see infection in you. Chlamydia. Lots of it."

Chlamydia is a term he has heard before. He isn't sure what it means either, but knows it's something dirty.

The girl hesitates for an instant, unsure how to react, then bursts out laughing. "Long-haired faggot's got *some* lip!" All the rest laugh too. The Firebird's engine revs and roars.

So does the El Camino's. The Kid gets up and crouches by his father's window, shakes the hair out of his eyes. "Race them, Dad. Blow them away."

His mother rolls up her window. "Nobody is racing anybody, for heaven's sake. They're drunk."

The Firebird's engine roars and roars. *"Do it,* Dad."

"Don't you *dare* do it," says his mother.

"Mary Lee," his father says. "Of course I'm not going to do it." He continues revving the engine, glares straight ahead. "I'm just waiting for the light."

Everything happens at once. The Kid looks at the stoplight and immediately sees how the x-ray glasses work—it is night that activates them!—sees that the red light has become a glowing red word in the fumy air: X-

111

RAY; X-RAY *twice,* one above the other, so that the lower mirrors the upper. The word turns green as he looks at it; it vibrates and rocks as the Camino vibrates and rocks—its back tires squealing, its engine howling. "Hold on, buddy," says his father, as the Kid grips the fender and the Camino launches forward, the Firebird doing likewise, the stench of scorched rubber wafting up and vanishing behind them, the g-force almost causing him to lose his grip, the wind savaging his hair, his mother shouting at his father, the streetlights flashing overhead, faster and faster, X-RAY—X-RAY—*X-RAY-X-RAY-XRAY!*

The cars blast neck and neck up East Trent Avenue, past the East Trent Motor-in (NOW PLAYING! BILLY JACK), past the House of Mai Tai Chinese Buffet ("We're So Proud of Our Food You Won't Believe It!"), until the sound of the Camino's engine blooms like a wet, black rose, opening wide, doubling in intensity, causing them to leap forward as though going into warp, leaving the Firebird behind, dazed, confused, weaving back and forth, the cones of its headlights lost in blue-tinged smoke, its headlights shouting X-RAY, all glittery yellow, cowardly yellow, signaling surrender.

112

The Firebird turns on Green Street, slinking away like a whipped dog. He looks into the rearview mirror and sees his father smiling, slapping the steering wheel; in the space of seconds he has transformed into a teenager, an adolescent; when he looks through the rear window he sees his mother has done the same, laughing, grinning broadly, her head thrown back, hair dancing, licking out the window, which she has rolled down again, the streetlights playing over her face, X-RAY, X-RAY, X-RAY.

And they just roll casually on up the road, past the neon bulldozer sign at Modern Machinery (with its animated treads like a Las Vegas marquee, the Golden Nugget, maybe, which he has seen destroyed on television by Glenn Langan as *The Colossal Man*), past the Futurist office building with the Modernistic panels along its pediment, past Spokane Community College and its big, bisected windows (he calls them *Reptilicus* windows because they are the same kind the monster escapes through in the movie), past the old Armour slaughterhouse where Uncle Shane worked in 1954, and where he'd learned to butcher his competitors to become a multi-millionaire, and which looms like the Bates

Mansion in the hazy dark—all the way to Spokane and beyond.

The Kid grins the whole way, lying upon his foam mattress, gazing at the stars and the moon, which says: X-RAY. He has seen the Camino transform into something previously unimaginable; a thing conflicted, repressed, angry—yet buoyant, exuberant, *free.* He, the Kid—now ten, but still a boy—has transformed too. He has become, for the first time, the Boy with the X-Ray Eyes. A surfer of invisible waves—explorer, reporter, seer—the boy who will put it all together.

X-Ray Rider.

THEY CELEBRATE THE VICTORY at a Chinese restaurant in downtown Spokane, at a little round table in a corner whose walls are comprised of glass. He has never seen his parents act quite this young or behave so affectionately toward each other, as though they have just met, as though they are the king and queen of the prom. They look like movie stars to him, their hair having been coifed by the wind, their skin tanned, and their teeth so straight and white. Everything is reflected in the shiny glass walls, beyond which cars glide back and forth: the

114

little orange candles—which are round and have little nets on them—the light with the wide-brimmed shade which hangs low over the table, himself. He is wearing his white Spiderman T-shirt with the blue trim, its sleeves rolled up like James Dean, and his brother's Little League baseball cap—black with a golden 'F,' for Frankenfurters. He has a belly full of scallops and snow crab, a pile of empty shells to make monsters, and the love of his parents, who are young, dashing, victorious. And he has a pair of X-ray glasses.

Nobody says anything about math or about bankruptcies. Instead his mother talks exuberantly about the future and what it holds, about how wonderfully he has learned to write and to draw; how another bid is just around the corner, that they will go to San Francisco and Los Angeles and San Diego and Las Vegas. That the external world holds no threat for a middle-class American family whose members are all healthy. That she has *faith*. That they have lots of time together. That they need be in no particular hurry; need not construct safety nets in case the center doesn't hold; need not belabor children over how to survive in the world.

It isn't until they have left and are several miles away that he realizes he has forgotten his X-ray glasses. He half shouts it in a cold panic, prompting his mother to order they turn around—which his father does, not too happy about it. The whole thing causes a bit of a row, with his father cursing and snapping out bitter words. The Kid cannot really blame him; it isn't as if this sort of thing hasn't happened before.

They drive all the way back—his father does, rather, while the Kid and his mother stare out the windows—and he runs in. The glasses are handed to him by a smiling waitress, who is cleaning their table. He takes them and slides them on. The effect is instantaneous: a hundred X-RAYs through the glass—neon signs, street lamps, the headlights of automobiles—all flashing and rotating and streaking, changing colors. They frame the waitress as if she were a goddess; make her positively beautiful—like one of the Mothra twins.

Only naked.

II | The Boy with the X-Ray Eyes

116

THE TRI-COLORED PHILLIPS 66 SIGNS and Sinclair logos with their green dinosaurs have all changed to the orange globes of Union 76 stations, like trees changing in autumn. He has lost the X-Ray glasses and found them again. There have been other changes. His father's work truck has been in and out of the shop, meaning the bed of the Camino is often full of five-gallon paint buckets. Often it is filled with more—sections of scaffolding, a blue-green compressor, brushes and rollers soaking in thinner, transmission fluid containers—everything splashed in paint, everything dirty. His father has been spending more time at home and more time in taverns. He drives the Camino to Seattle most weekends, looking for work but invariably calling home, causing his mother to run her hands through her hair and say, "Why don't you head on back." A yellow bandage over a cotton ball may be seen when she does this. When asked about it she tells him that she has been donating blood.

They head out to Coeur d'Alene, Idaho, ostensibly to see the hydroplanes. They won't be racing or anything— it is evening, after all—but his father thinks they might find some down by the bay, just moored in the moonlight. He wants to show the Kid (who has had a

117

hydroplane fixation since hearing Sheldon describe them as "jet-boats") what they look like. They don't see any, but a man walking along the pier tells them that there are some in Sandpoint, about 40 miles northeast, as part of a traveling exhibition.

To get there they have to cross what his mother calls "The Longest Bridge," a two-mile-long road on stilts that traverses the northernmost end of Lake Pend Oreille—a lake so vast and deep, says his father, the U.S. Navy uses it to test submarines. For the Kid, the notion of a two-mile-long bridge over that kind of depth is awe-inspiring, even if he isn't sure what constitutes a mile. His mother (who has a gift for showmanship and can make even the most mundane thing seem novel and thrilling) adds to this awe, making hyperbolic pronouncements as they approach the bridge.

"Here it comes," she says as they draw near. "Look, Sweetie! We're about to go over *The Longest Bridge!*"

By the time they clack over the entry point and onto the bridge, he is primed for any manner of wonderment: a road which rolls like a rollercoaster, a glimpse of something swimming beneath the surface—a surviving plesiosaur, even, as in Loch Ness?—a glimpse of a

118

Polaris submarine's conning tower... Instead he sees only blackness, and the yellow-orange lights of the homes and businesses along the far banks.

Yet there is something hypnotic about their passage over the black lake. The distant, glittering lights, the wavering, moonlit water, and the drone of the radials combined with the *clackity-clack!* each time they pass over the joints between prefabricated sections, create an aura of reverie. His mother turns on the radio and begins humming along with Johnny Cash, whom she normally doesn't like. He is singing "Ring of Fire." The Kid opens his magazine. Dad just whistles into oblivion, which is typical.

He opens to a picture of a sweat-soaked Doc Savage, the fabled Man of Bronze, from the movie of the same name. He has piercing, steely-blue eyes and fair, shortly cropped hair. He is wearing a Khaki shirt ripped open nearly to the waist (where a massive sidearm gleams), and German soldier-type trousers tucked into tall, black boots. He is standing at the rail of a ship—or a nuclear submarine—a shining bronze (but really Idealized White) action-figure, the Aryan Nephilim.

He shows the picture to his mother.

119

"That's what you'll look like someday," she says.

He stares at the picture for the longest time, lost in his own cathedral. So that's what he'll be, after all: a commanding officer—for that's what the man is, clearly—a "Doctor," even. A Leader of Men. Yet, though he is elated that he will grow up to be such a specimen, that he will grow taller—which in fact he has begun to do—more muscular; that he will overcome his shyness and indecision and cowardice, he finds the idea unsettling also. For her words suggest he will *change,* which implies she and Dad will change, will age, and so will the world.

He listens to the road and imagines that the El Camino is in fact a time machine, that each *clackity-clack!* represents a decade traversed forward or back in time. He becomes so enthralled by the notion that he gropes for his X-Ray glasses and dives across his mother, hanging head and shoulders out the window, peering into the void, the wind whipping his hair which lashes his face—attempting to see the water but seeing only the dull green guardrail, and beyond that, space. He strains and strains, but with no lights to assist him, he cannot penetrate the darkness.

120

"You're going to keep it up until you lose those," says his mother. He feels her curl a finger through one of his belt loops. He clasps his hands to his temples, securing the paper glasses. In fact he has resolved to never lose them again. He raises his head, looks through the lenses at the lights across the lake, each of which instantly becomes the word X-RAY—a train of X-RAYS, marching parallel to them but in the opposite direction. Out here he can really hear the *clackity-clacking*—but it isn't just tires against the bridge. It is the sound he heard while lying on the floor by the cement quarry and by the store where he'd picked out his first comic book; the sound of a failing transmission, yes, but also Johnny Cash playing on the Motorola, singing, *"Oh, it burns, burns, burns…the ring of fire…the ring of fire."* The sound of swarming yellow jackets and flapping sheets, swishing swings, pounding pistons. A sound coming from everywhere at once and from everything, not just the bowels of the Camino—a sound so dense and deep that it sinks through the floor of the car and becomes far away again. A sound with individual parts until you hear it from out here, going this fast, where it

121

becomes a single whirring entity, a roar at the heart of the universe.

THEY DRIVE AROUND SANDPOINT for what seems like hours, but don't see any hydroplanes. Finally, in the spring of 1978, he sees his first "jet boat." It is during a matinee-showing of Sun Classic Pictures' *The Mysterious Monsters* at the Garland Theater in west Spokane. The movie is a documentary about Bigfoot and the Loch Ness Monster and is narrated by Peter Graves, who introduces a loop of grainy, black and white footage purporting to show a speeding jet boat being destroyed by an unidentified object beneath the surface of Loch Ness.

His brother, who in the fall will begin high school as the Kid begins junior high, balks as he starts the Camino (he has a learning permit to drive so long as their father is in the car, which he is, having dropped them off and returned). "That could have been anything—it could have been a school of fish, for all you know."

The Kid is unmoved. "A jet-boat would have cut through fish like butter."

"Easy does it," says their father.

122

"Not at that velocity," says his brother. "A penny dropped from the Empire State Building will bore into *concrete.*" He laughs as he backs from the slot, "Shows what you know."

"Watch out, Sheldon," says their father.

"I know you look stupid in those red velvet hippie pants—"

"Watch out, Sheldon!"

There is a *crunch* as Sheldon backs into another car—not hard, merely a tap. They all turn around, see a maroon Volkswagen Beetle being driven by a twenty-something woman in a blue halter top and wide-brimmed hat. She has long, straight hair the color of shredded wheat and is the prettiest girl the Kid has ever seen. She is giving them all the finger.

"All right now *goddammit,*" says their father. "See what happens when you don't pay attention…"

Everyone gathers between the vehicles, inspects the damage. It isn't horrible—the Camino's rear quarter panel has sustained a minor dent, which is smeared with maroon. The Beetle looks the same only inversed. The damage is so minor, in fact, that the woman tells them to never mind, and quickly climbs back into her car—peeling from the lot with an acidic chirp.

Their father stares at the quarter panel, hands on his hips. "Well, it could have been worse. But a first dent is a first dent. That'll rust."

HIS SUMMER SCHOOL TEACHER, Mr. Booker, has a special treat for the class. He is impressed overall with the quality of the students' creative writing assignments, and wants to use one in particular to illustrate the day's topic—which shall remain a secret until after "the treat." Mr. Booker is a short, stocky, dark-eyed man who always wears Hawaiian shirts, and whose black hair curls against his forehead like Superman's. He isn't one of the Kid's favorites—those are almost invariably the women—but the Kid has a certain respect for him, as do the rest of the students, because he is young and good-looking, by adult standards, and no nicknames seem to apply to him as they do other teachers, names such as "Keg-legs Monahan" or "Butt-lips Cooligan." Booker can always be relied upon to wander far a field of the topic, as when he gets dreamy-eyed about his high school days—which he does about every two weeks—and says,

124

"They'll be the best days of your lives. *The best days of your lives.*"

Mr. Booker presents a sheaf of papers, hitches his Khakis an inch, and sits on the edge of his desk. "The assignment, as you know, was to write a prologue, but to write it in such a way that it reflects the entire story. I think we have someone here who has done just that. That, and so much more."

The Kid stiffens. He knows what's coming. He doesn't know how he knows it, but he knows it, and it thrills him. It thrills him because he has found something he can do well besides draw—which he enjoys but is slow at—which compliments his drawing, works in tandem with it, as when he draws comics, so that he owns it, all of it. So that he is beholden to no one's whim but his own—is a businessperson, in a sense, like his parents. Has his own equipment, his own scaffolding and compressor, works for no one.

It thrills him too because Jenny will be listening, Jenny who sits kitty-corner from him in the back of the room—Jenny with the pug nose and the freckles beneath her eyes, the sharp chin, the tallish forehead—Jenny whose wheat-colored hair frames her face just so, whose

125

shoulders are small and square, whose arms are strong-looking like a boy's, who wears an Indian arrowhead on a leather string around her neck and never makes fun of him, not for being skinny or having platinum hair like an albino or a crooked front tooth or anything. That Jenny.

Mr. Booker clears his throat and gives the sheaf of papers a snap, like a newspaper. "'The Boy with the X-Ray Eyes,' by Wayne K. Spitzer. Once upon a time in 1978, in an elm-dark town with lots of grain elevators and dim orange streetlamps, there lived a boy who had X-ray eyes. Almost nothing about this boy was remarkable other than he had X-ray eyes, though he could draw reasonably well and bore a striking resemblance to the crinkly-antennaed ant from *The Ant and the Aardvark,* and not just because he had cowlicks."

A few muted laughs, nice laughs, not hostile. Jenny and two others, a girl and a boy. His heart races.

"But he did have X-ray eyes, and he used them, as would any boy, to see what he was going to get for Christmas, or to cheat on math tests, or to see what all the most popular girls looked like naked."

A small uproar—some snickers but mostly approval. He doesn't move an inch. Doesn't breathe.

126

"But as he grew up his X-ray vision became more acute, so that he came to see not just through clothes and skin but through the walls of the world itself. Indeed, he came to see through to the center of time and space, where he saw something that terrified him, something whose tentacles—for that's what they seemed—*reached the corners of creation.*" He emphasizes this part, for dramatic effect, then leans forward, scanning the room, making eye contact with everyone. "And it saw him. This of course was so startling to the boy that he died instantly, though he continued to wander the earth as a ghost for many years—a dead boy walking. He got excited about something once in a while, and threw himself into bursts of activity, but mostly he just went through the motions, and, as a ghost can spawn no offspring, continued to fade until at last he was no more, white sheet, chains and all. Yet the ghost never forgot the boy, and before he faded away he set about telling the boy's story, having come to the belief—in his years wandering the earth—that, beyond the particulars, this was really every boy's story, and every girl's too. This, then, is the story of the Boy with the X-ray Eyes. A boy that time almost forgot, but didn't. A boy who saw too

127

much, went too high, and finally fell to earth. It opens with the Universal International logo, the one that comes before movies such as *The Mole People* and *The Creature from the Black Lagoon.* It closes with an enormous explosion and the boy's death and the end of his world, an end he saw coming while it was still way out in space-time, because he had X-ray eyes. The end."

The room erupts in applause, like something from a television program, everyone clapping, turning and looking at him, faces red and jolly, smiles showing white. He has no idea how to react, how to respond. He is not one of the popular kids. What does one do? How does one behave in such a situation—where does one place one's eyes? He tries placing them on Jenny but her shining gaze is too much, her smile too broad, her straight teeth too white. He is not worthy of that gaze. He could save the world, cure disease, end all war, and still he would not be worthy of that gaze. Who could be?

Mr. Booker is clapping too, pages flapping back and forth in his hand, like the wings of a bird. "Yeah," he says, nodding. "You bet. Let's hear it. Why don't you all stand up."

128

Everyone stands, the legs of their desks squeaking. They clap and clap and clap. At last Booker says, "All right, all right..." He spreads his arms, gestures, *Down, down.* Everyone sits down. Mr. Booker holds up the sheaf of papers, squints. "Pretty good, pretty good. Listen to some of these: 'Elm-dark...crinkly-antennaed...*the corners of creation.* Amazing for a twelve-year-old— more like something you'd read in a book. A *real* book..." He picks up the paperback on his desk, *The Lord of the Flies* by William Golding. "Like this one."

He tosses the paperback back onto his desk, then holds the sheaf of papers at eye-level. He rotates them horizontally, places his thumb and forefingers at the center, and rips. Then he lays the halves together and rips again. He lays the quarters together and rips again. Then he tosses the stack into the wastebasket and says, "Today we're going to talk about plagiarism."

III | The Dead Wasps

HIS HEART IS RACING; there is nothing he can do about it. The plagiarism discussion has ended, at last, but it has ended the way it begun—with a cruel flourish. Mr.

129

Booker has handed him a sealed envelope to be given directly to his parents, handed it to him in front of everyone, which has elicited from some a sound even worse than snickers—gasps. Mr. Booker is setting up the 16mm projector. He watches as Booker removes the spool from a wide, flat canister and hangs the spool on an arm of the projector, flicks the switch. The projector hums to life and he begins threading the film, which rattles through the gate like a mini Gatling gun. "Billy, if you'll get the lights," says Mr. Booker.

The Kid sits in the dark still too stunned to move, fingering the envelope. He does not know what someone would have to do to deserve what has just happened; to be used as a prop by Mr. Booker, this man who is so much older than him and so much bigger, who is the Teacher, whose job it is to treat everybody equally and with respect, whose job is to *teach,* not to pile on like a twelve-year-old bully. And he *has* been piled on, everyone in the class having turned and looked at least once, even Jenny, who looked at him as though he were a horse with a broken leg—whom may have to be shot—when Booker talked about the dire consequences of copying another's work, of the humiliating fate awaiting

130

such shameless literary thieves. He looks around as the movie begins, slips the envelope into his notebook.

What troubles him, what vexes him completely, is Booker's feckless assumption that he has copied something at all, because he hasn't, not a word, at least not that he is aware of. He has *drawn* on something—*X: The Man with the X-Ray Eyes*—but that isn't the same as copying, or is it? What troubles him is that Booker can frame him any way he likes, can title him, like a book. You are this, Wayne K. Spitzer. You are not what you think you are, but what *I* say you are. What troubles him is the suspicion that Mr. Booker is only the teenager in the Firebird, grown up. But what troubles him *the most,* what troubles him beyond all these, what defeats him utterly and finally, is that he did not see it coming. That he was the last to know. That perhaps it was a cruel joke all along and that everyone was in on it, even Jenny and the boy who laughed nicely— everyone, that is, except him.

Since the second half of the class is about health and fitness, the film talks about the human body and how everything works. It isn't a Sex Ed film, though the basics are covered, which causes much snickering, as when they were discussing plagiarism and looking back at him. Two images in the film lay spells upon him, one like a charm and the other like a curse. The first is a shot of the human brain while dreaming as viewed through a special lens, so that thoughts themselves light up like little freeways at night, like whole cities. The second is a shot of a human torso undergoing open-heart surgery, its chest cut open like a fish, the flesh pinned back with clamps, everything draped with green sterile cloth, except the heart cavity itself, where a red-black heart beats—defiantly, it seems—while the cardiogram scribbles spikes and bloodied white- gloves exchange bloodied, stainless steel instruments. Nonetheless, when he sees his parents pull up outside the classroom window, his first thought isn't about the beating heart, or the envelope, or telling his mother about what has happened. It's, *That's not the right car.*

AS THEY DRIVE to the garage in the big Ford station wagon, he doesn't mention the incident or the envelope, though he has dutifully handed it over and can clearly see it laying on the dash. He is in a daze from everything in general, the incident with Booker, the red-black beating

132

heart, riding in a car that is not the Camino—the fact that he is not only failing Booker's class but his summer math class as well. Nor does he ask about the ball of cotton taped to the crook of his mother's arm, or why everyone is so silent, or why his dad won't let go of his mother's hand—even when he clearly needs to in order to drive. Besides, his mother would only say, *'We'll* worry about the driving, honey. *You* worry about your funny book.'

"They only took about six," she says finally.

"Christ, Mary Lee," his father says. "I'm not thinking about the *money.*"

He can see his mother's profile from the back seat— she is staring out the window, face reflected in the glass. Her skin is pale and puffy, her eyes vacant. The treetops slide over her like water.

She says nothing more until they reach Benny's Car Clinic and are bouncing through the dirt lot. "I don't know why you brought it *here,*" she says.

"SHE'S FUCKED UP pretty bad," says the man with a droopy mustache who greets them at the roll-up, and he sees his mother's face flush, not with embarrassment but anger. She doesn't say anything but he knows what she is

133

thinking: *Mind not dropping four-letter words in front of my kid?* She leans close and whispers, "Why don't you go wait for us in the station wagon?"

"Sure," he says, and trots back to the wagon. He climbs in and rolls down his window. He watches them walk into the garage together. "Watch the tranny fluid," says the man with the mustache.

He stares at the open door. He can still hear the man with the mustache talking, as well as his father, but can't tell what they are saying. His mother is silent. He stares at the door until it is clear they will not be coming out soon, and then lies down. He rolls his head on the vinyl, stares between the front seats at the empty forward cabin of the wagon. The chromed column-shifter and radio gleam; the consul clock ticks monotonously. He listens to the adults' voices echoing inside the garage, trying to pick out individual words, until a metal door rolls up and an engine revs, and he loses them in a clamor of riveting.

THEY HAVE DINNER early, before it has begun to get dark. He sits at the dining room table listlessly, alternating his attention between the cars passing silently back and forth on Mission Avenue and the doorway to

134

the kitchen, beyond which, just out of view, his father and brother are helping his mother with dinner. His brother looks at him from around the corner every few minutes, but jerks away whenever their eyes meet. The Kid asks again if he can help but is told no, that it's a surprise.

At last his father calls, "Okay, buddy, close your eyes!"

He closes his eyes, understanding instantly. They are celebrating his thirteenth birthday—three days away, on July 15—early. He had not exactly forgotten about it but has not been thinking about it much either. What does one want when they are thirteen? He has not quite figured that out yet.

When he opens his eyes there is an enormous home-made pizza in front of him, the kind with the deep-dish crust, topped with thirteen candles but topped also, though only on one side, with anchovies, his favorite. Everyone sings 'Happy Birthday' and he blows out the candles. Afterwards, when they have eaten and opened the presents, which are modest compared to years passed, and everyone has settled into pretty much routine conversation, his mother says, "I think we made the right

135

decision in just having this one serviced. Four-hundred dollars! That car is a decade old, for Pete's sake."

"Mmm," says his father. "It'll be a classic someday, though. We'll have to do it eventually."

Sheldon laughs, nicely, insincerely. "You've probably already spent that much on tranny fluid."

"Sorry," says their mother. "Until we can win a bid, this transmission will have to do."

His father dabs the corners of his mouth, stands. "The public schools are coming up." He gathers some of the dishes, heads into the kitchen. "We'll just have to hope for the best."

"That's worked well," says Sheldon. He picks up the remaining dishes, follows their father into the kitchen.

The Kid and his mother look at each other across the table. She does not look well.

"Here's how it's going to be," she says. "I'm calling your principal on Monday. You are to be put into a room all by yourself and given nothing but a legal pad and some pencils. You're going to write a story, which you will then hand directly to the principal. Are you prepared to accept this mission, Lieutenant Spitzer?"

The Kid doesn't say anything, waiting for more. When no more is forthcoming he says, "I am— Lieutenant Spitzer is, sir. Ma'am. Sir. However, the lieutenant…. Permission to speak bluntly, sir."

His mother raises an eyebrow. "Permission granted."

It all comes at once. "Sir, the lieutenant has been less than forthcoming about his fitness to be—lieutenant. Not his fitness to write but his fitness to work mathematical equations. It is the lieutenant's belief he will not be ready to graduate with his class—with or without this test of artistry. The lieutenant also believes his commanding officer has been less than forthcoming with *him,* thus compromising his fitness and well-being. The lieutenant has reason to believe he has been left out of the loop, and should be debriefed *thoroughly* before further action is taken. Sir."

His mother leans back in her chair, which creaks and groans—studies him. The grandfather clock in the living room ticks. "Petition denied," she says. She pushes her chair back, stands. "The lieutenant is still only twelve years old. That'll be all."

137

IT IS TWILIGHT. He mounts the cool rungs of the step-ladder, flashlight in hand, and peers into his window well. Because the concrete cavity has been covered with wooden slats it is all but impenetrable to the naked eye, with only a few shafts of twilight peeking between boards, and even these swallowed instantly by the well's total blackness.

He presses the red plastic lens hood of the flashlight flush against the glass but does not turn it on. It will be a matter of concentration, he knows. A matter of *imaginative* concentration—like drawing pictures. It will require that he move the flashlight slowly away from the glass, causing the X-RAY effect. It will require that he see and comprehend the first layer before extrapolating that onto a second, then a third, and a fourth. It will require that he *imagine* as hard as he can, that he give himself over to the one thing he *knows* he owns.

He pulls the X-ray glasses from his back pocket and opens the cardboard frames; they have aged since 1976 and are truly thin as paper, creased. He slides them on and adjusts them over his ears, pushes them flush against the bridge of his nose. He closes his eyes and counts to ten, thumbs on the flashlight. When he opens them he

138

will have X-ray vision. At first, of course, there will be nothing. But then he'll begin peeling back the layers: first the outermost shell, then the intermediary layers, then the first layer of hex comb, finally he will see the bees themselves—my God!—crawling in and out of the comb, flopping over each other's thoraxes, ticking. But he must not push too fast nor *imagine* too hard—like Dr. Xavier—lest he penetrate the hive's very heart. Lest he see something horrifying, something fat and white and terrible, something vital, brutal, beautiful—the queen bee herself, perhaps, luminescent in the dark—shifting and glowing from within. Lest he find, deeper still, "The eye—that sees *all!*"

He opens his eyes.

The hive is there, a banded, misshapen gas planet—Neptune, perhaps, only gray—in the spill of the flashlight. There are no signs of activity; the bees are all out on their rounds, pollinating flowers, swarming kids. The thought thrills him. He holds the flashlight against the glass, looks around the well. It looks like the pit the sailors fall into in the 1933 version of King Kong; everything hung with hammocks of spider web, sides covered in creeper vines and moss, its floor piled with dead branches and broken sections of window frame, some tangled storm screen. He is moving the flashlight away when he notices shapes amidst the cobwebs and along the molding—yellow jackets, like little black seashells, lying upon backs and sides and stomachs, legs and antennae akimbo.

They are all dead. He looks at the nest, notices for the first time its paleness, its lifelessness, like the moon. Sees it is merely a ghost town of ashen, papery layers, some of which have completely disintegrated, exposing black, collapsed comb. The hive itself is dead—has been, it seems clear to him now, for years. The only living thing in the window well, the only thing with any color, is the flashlight's reflection—X-RAY—a mere mirage, which burns at the center of the hive. That and himself, *his* reflection, itself only visible because of the light.

IV | Fire Not Flames

SOMETHING HAS HAPPENED. Something beyond the attack by Booker, beyond the beating red-black heart. He has come across an audio cassette, something he recorded at the Starlight Drive-in, years ago. It is a

140

recording of a *Pink Panther* cartoon and some concessions ads, and part of a western movie, the name of which he cannot remember. In the recording he can hear Clint Eastwood and some other actor talking confrontationally amidst a commotion; he doesn't recall what the commotion was— but can hear shouting and gunfire in the background. What interests him, however, is an almost silent stretch near the end, a stretch where nothing much can be heard, only stealthy footsteps on stones, a stretch that must have been recorded right before the batteries died. In the stretch he thinks he hears his mother's voice—distorted, barely audible through the white noise—but clear enough to pick out some words, something about white blood cell counts and low-grade dysphasia, about red flags and warning signals, increased testing, additional x-rays. He is certain that he hears one word in particular that he has not heard in years. The word is 'carcinoma.'

HIS MOTHER HAS BEEN admitted to Sacred Heart Medical Center. He is told this by his father and Fast Eddy while sitting on Eddy's back deck in east Spokane, a deck made of stained planks which supports a hot tub

141

and a wet bar and has a roof and walls made of lattice wood, which are strung with Christmas lights and paper lanterns so that everything resembles a low-rent Tiki bar. Although he wants to speak to her right away his father tells him that the hospital is closed to visitors from 7 pm to 9 pm while the staff does their "change of shift report," and that she'll only be there a day or two anyway while they run some tests, though his father is going up again tonight to take her some books. In fact he excuses himself much earlier than that, having only had one beer to Eddy's four, and leaves without so much as looking at the Kid, which he supposes ought to offend him but doesn't, because there really isn't that much to say. Without his mother to connect them they are strangers.

"Here," says Fast Eddy, after seeing his father off and returning from the bar, and hands the Kid a can of RC, which Eddy has retrieved from the ice chest so that its sides run with water and pieces of frost. Eddy settles into his lawn chair and stares at the yard, which he's transformed into a Japanese-style garden with bubbling fountains and lightscaped waterfalls and a brook winding around a Buddha—which he has more of in the basement, as well as oversized frogs and toadstools and garden gnomes, all lined up like the Terracotta Army (which the Kid has seen pictures of in *National Geographic*), but which he's bought cheap in Mexico and plans to sell for a profit in Spokane. He hooks a finger beneath the pull ring of his can and tears it open, drops the ring into his ashtray. "You know how long I've known your father?" He doesn't look at him as he says this, only stares straight ahead at the water garden.

The Kid hooks a finger beneath the ring of his can, tears it open, drops the ring into Eddy's ashtray. He stares at the water garden also.

"Since '62—the year President Kennedy said we were going to the moon. I met him even before he met your mother—at Eddie Murphy's Tavern in Hillyard. Good old Eddie's, how's that for symmetry?"

The Kid sips his RC, imagining the scene in his head, directing it like a movie, fading up on the illuminated sign outside Eddie Murphy's—with its crossed bats and baseball, everything in black and white—craning to street level and up to the window as Fast Eddy goes in and sits next to his father. "He must have been about my age, twenty-nine, thirty, something like that. Nice-looking fellow—looked like Steve

143

McQueen. But what I remember most was the contrast, because he was so impeccably dressed and his hair was slicked back and his shoes were shined, yet it seemed as though he hadn't eaten or slept or bathed in days. And I asked him about it—partly out of genuine curiosity but partly just to be a smart-ass, because I liked the sound of my own voice then, liked being a smart-ass, I still had front teeth, see, to be a smart-ass with, and I said, 'How ya feeling, Slick?'

"Now, there are men you can say that to and those you can't. And I didn't know which type your father was—which I suppose was half the fun. But I remember he shook a cigarette from his pack and placed it between his lips, and flipped his lighter open, but didn't ignite it, and told me about finding a firecracker when he was a boy which he mistook for a cigarette even though it was colored bright orange, and about lighting it, one-handed, waving the match out real cool, just like he'd seen his father do, and waving his Zippo as he repeated it, like he might curl his fist around it any moment, adding, 'And I just sucked that orange fag and watched its tip sparkle and hiss and smoke until its fuse burned to the stub and everything just *exploded,* right in my face.'"

144

The Kid looks at Fast Eddy, who takes a drag off his cigarette, his face lighting orange, and blows blue smoke through his nostrils.

"Now, I may not have had much of a formal education, but I was sober and what he'd said and how he'd said it sounded an awful lot to me like the preamble to a punch in the face, so I slid off my stool and told him I didn't want any trouble, that I'd just been fooling with him, and could I buy him a beer because frankly it looked like he could use one, not to mention a good meal. And we became chums, because he was and still is the type of man you can say that to. And he went on to tell me about what the firecracker had done, which was to nearly blow his teeth out and to rip his lips open, but that he'd had to wait nearly an hour before going to the hospital because his father balked at the idea of a bill, suggesting his mother could take him if she wanted to pay for it, which she didn't, at least not until she realized the extent of the damage—although she had to change outfits first and fix her hair."

The Kid stares at Fast Eddy and takes a sip. Fast Eddy looks back at him. "This life you've had so far, this

145

childhood, it ain't your father's childhood, see. Ain't your mother's either." He gets up. "Let's walk."

The Kid gets up and they walk.

"See, he'd only recently moved back to Spokane from Seattle, where he and his brothers had been working for their father—Spitzer and Sons Painting—at Boeing Field, making lots of money. Or at least someone was making lots of money—Giff didn't seem to think he was seeing his share, even though they were all supposed to be equal partners. But your father just did the work, see, the physical work, and some of the estimating and bidding. It was his eldest brother who handled all the books and was sort of the comptroller of the whole operation."

"Uncle Shane," says the Kid.

"Right. Not your Uncle Lew."

Eddy leads him along a narrow stone path through the garden. "So there was always that, plus the normal sibling rivalry and the fact that old man Spitzer sort of encouraged it, because that was what had always worked for him—boost productivity by pitting workers against each other, for bonuses, titles, whatever. The problem was that your father and Uncle Shane weren't just

146

employees but co-owners and brothers—brothers with very different temperaments."

Eddy crouches by the fish pond, running his fingertips through it, making little ripples. "Check this out." The Kid crouches next to him and gazes into the water. "Got a little bit of everything, goldfish, carp, bluegills, rosy red minnows. See how the light makes the water glow? Like they're swimming through air." The Kid watches the fish weave in and out of the water lilies and each other, but also notices how they wheel off occasionally as a group, pivoting in unison, undulating as a single animal, like an eel. "This pond attracts all sorts of things, birds, garter snakes, frogs. Caught a salamander out here the other night—got it in a little cage in my kitchen. I'll show it to you before you go. Been feedin' it lettuce."

The pond is scattered with water-hyacinths and irises which skitter away as the Kid touches the surface. Fast Eddy stands. "Tough customers, your grandfather and your Uncle Shane..." He laughs bitterly. "Not the type you want to go up to in a tavern and call 'Slick.' For men like that it's all about the game, the fight, the purse. It may have been a family business but they weren't in it

147

for family. You don't get as far as they do without…without having a demonic sublime. Your father now, he wasn't like that. Not then. All he wanted, I think, was a real family."

He starts moving again. The Kid shakes the water from his hand and follows.

"So when the contract was over and there was no more work they came home to Spokane. But there was no work here either—at least not in your Uncle Shane's estimation; because he was the one who kept his ear to the ground and could divan these things. He had a knack for it, see, probably because he was a gambler, like your grandfather—Poker, mainly. Texas Hold 'Em. I reckon your Uncle Lew's played a game or two also. It was about this time that Shane suggested folding the company for good, that your father might benefit from withdrawing his share completely and starting his own business, which Shane would help him with by giving him his portion of the physical assets—scaffolding, spray guns, that sort of thing—because he was thinking about going into a different business altogether."

Eddy pauses at a spot where the elephant ear plants encroach on the path, holding a frond so that it doesn't strike the Kid in the face. The Kid steps through and Eddy lets it go. They walk back to their lawn chairs.

"Well, see, your father looked up to Shane, rivalry or no, and took his advice, and before your dad knew it he was out—out of the company and out of Spokane, because he fell for some Eskimo girl he met downtown, and I mean really fell, and took a Greyhound bus with her back to Anchorage, figuring he'd come back for his equipment later and start a new life with her in Alaska, maybe even homestead some land."

Eddy collapses in his lawn chair, exhaling, as the Kid stands and listens. "That lasted maybe five or six months, until he came home one day and she had her ass in the air like a housecat being scratched—with the neighbor fella doing the scratching, see—and he ditched out to Anchorage International and spent everything he had on a plane ticket home, leaving Alaska exactly how he came, with nothing."

The Kid tips his can to his lips and empties it, then scrunches it in his hand. He tosses it into the wastebasket, thinking about the Eskimo girl's ass, imagining the curve of her olive-skinned back, like the upright lid of a Baby Grand Piano.

149

"Of course no one would pick him up at the airport, because it wasn't that type of family. So he dialed a painter friend who had worked with him for his father—Dale Benner, I think—who offered to let him flop at his place in Hillyard and came out to get him. That's when he found out that his brother hadn't gone into 'a different business altogether,' but in fact had sued his father over a portion of the Boeing profits and established his own company, Shane T. Spitzer Painting, and had won the bid for the refurbishment of Fairchild Air Force Base, which was going to be huge, bigger, by far, than the Boeing deal.

"And finally, after telling the whole story, your father turned to me and said, 'How do I feel? Well, I've gone from the girl, the gold watch, and everything—to a bag of clothes, a toothbrush, and enough money for this beer.' Then he laughed and said, 'I guess I feel like that firecracker just blew up in my face again.'"

FAST EDDY LIGHTS A FRESH CIGARETTE, the glow of the flame turning his whole face orange. "Now, why do you suppose I told you that?"

The Kid just looks at him.

150

"I told you that because that had been the worst moment in your father's life so far. He wasn't old, but he wasn't young either—thirty ain't twenty no matter how much they say. Thirty is when you realize how much time you've wasted and that you better get moving— while fearing deep down that it's already too late. I told you that because, as bad as things were for your father at that instant, as desperate and hungry and lonely and hopeless as he was, I walked by the window of Eddie Murphy's the next day and saw him seated in a booth with the most beautiful woman I had ever seen. I mean, this woman looked like Lucille Ball—not the one from *The Lucy Show* or even *I Love Lucy with Desi Arnaz*— more like the one from *Stage Door;* with her hair bobbed around the back and coifed on one side, wearing a blue cocktail dress with one of those mandarin collars, and a blue cap, the netting of which sort of veiled her face. And there was the Giffer, looking pretty dapper for a penniless drifter, I thought— chatting her up, holding her hand across the table, both of them laughing—as though neither had a care in the world.

"Course they saw me gawking through the window—how couldn't they? They were seated right on the other side of the glass; and Giff gestured for me to come in, which I did, and sat next to him. That was the first time I ever saw your mother, Mary Lee, and she had lines of grace that day, let me tell you. But she had a demonic sublime too. I don't know if Giff could see it but I saw it right away— in the way she held her chin down and looked up at him through the veil of her hat. Know what a demonic sublime is?"

The Kid shakes his head.

"It's something hidden, an electrical current say, which actuates something else. A necessary imperfection…" Eddy puts a fist to his chest, stifles a belch. His eyes are bloodshot and rummy. "Lines of grace…. Regardless, I knew right away the spark had met the gas, and that your father's life was going to change—*bang-bang-bang,* like that."

The Kid continues looking at him.

"Sheldon, Kym, you—*bang-bang-bang,* like that. I guess what I'm trying to say is, there's ebb and flow to everything…everything breathes. It's like I told you years ago, when your father brought home the Camino. The sparks push down the pistons and drive the crankshaft. The El Camino breathes; see, just like a person. The ocean breathes. But the breathing is different from the thing itself…" Eddy drains the last of his beer and stares at the little round candle on the table, which in fact is a big wooden spool he has brought home from the job site and lain upon its side—picks the candle up. "Now what do you suppose I have in my hand?"

The Kid looks at the candle, the actual wick of which he cannot see, only its glow. "A candle."

"That's right. So what's a candle?"

"Something made of wax, with a wick inside it. You light the wick and get a flame—"

"A flame!" Eddy slaps his hands together. "That's right." He turns the candle this way and that. "Or is it? Okay, let's call it a flame. Now—is that a noun or a verb?"

The Kid crosses his eyes at him. "Both."

"Sure…it's an action *and* a thing."

"Right."

Eddy blows the candle out, sets it back on the table. "Now what is it?"

The Kid watches a little wisp of smoke rise, and then looks at Eddy. "It's nothing. You blew it out."

"The action or the thing?"

153

"Both."

"So what are those?" He points at the candles along the bar.

The Kid hesitates. "Candles—flames." He looks at Eddy, who shakes his head. *"Fire,"* he quickly adds.

"Bravo!" says Eddy, grinning. "And not just there but everywhere. All throughout Spokane. So I didn't blow out fire." He frowns suddenly. "What did I blow out then?"

The Kid looks back at the candles; then at the painting mounted above them, which depicts geometric shapes, a row of women, he thinks, descending a staircase.

Eddy laughs. "Think about it." He gets up, groaning. "Meanwhile, let's find a container. Because I've got a salamander without a boy—for a boy without a salamander."

V | The Giant Spider Invasion

THIS IS IT. *The Food of the Gods,* about which he has read so much, has come to town: it is playing at the East Sprague Drive-in Theater, the second feature in a triple-

154

bill which includes *Empire of the Ants* and *The Giant Spider Invasion*. They head out after Walter Cronkite and the local news, which, because it is a slow news day, is full of nothing but generalized doom: sun flares heating the top layers of Earth's atmosphere and increasing the drag on Skylab—America's abandoned space station—potentially causing it to fall anywhere, even Spokane; the U.S. Geological Survey predicting earthquakes and a possible eruption at Mount St. Helens, only a few hundred miles away; illegal aliens coming up from Mexico, from Haiti, from California, as well as Africanized killer bees.

With so much doom in the air and the theater drawing nearer, the Kid feels giddy, maniacal. He ignores his brother who is in the bed of the Camino with him, his arm propped on the opposite fender, and instead watches the streetlamps, which shout X-RAY, X-RAY, X-RAY....

He is becoming a different being behind the glasses. Behind the glasses he is becoming ultra-human—an agent of Divine Will—with an agenda having nothing to do with humans. Behind the glasses he has started work toward an inscrutable end that he himself does not understand. There is an incredible power and energy in there, in those oily black lenses. A bass hum. Something *moving,* which races and burns. But there is something else too. Something immutable, solid, like a planet light-years away which scientists recognize only by the echoes it makes through space-time. An asteroid in the wormhole. It cannot be seen yet but it can be sensed.

It is out there. It is on the horizon. It is coming.

"You look like a douche bag in those," says Sheldon as they pull into the East Sprague Drive-in, late. They have had to stop at Zip Trip for tranny fluid. The Kid just looks at him. He doesn't know what to make of Sheldon either—this new brother who wears gold polyester shirts with stiff collars and pointy lapels, like garden trowels—clamshell necklaces, feathered hair. Who has transformed into Leif Garret seemingly overnight—like in a horror movie; like Lon Chaney turning into the Wolfman in fast-motion. He doesn't understand why Sheldon has even come. He is old enough now to drive himself; has a job at Taco Time, his own money. He even has a car, a 1970 Fire-bird, which their father is helping him pay off. But they've been going everywhere together lately, his family; everything

156

old is new again—including a black leather-bound Bible which his mother used to tote to Sunday services but which now lies on the Camino's dash.

Everyone honks as the beams of the Camino's headlamps sweep across the screen. Through her open window he hears his mother say, *"Away* they go!" and laugh. "You'd think the world was at an end."

He looks at the screen as his father kills the headlights and backs into a stall—takes off the X-ray glasses—sees black ants carrying disproportionably large yellow petals across steppes of chipped bark. As his father sets up the speaker the Kid hears an authoritative voice intone: "Have you ever taken a *good, close look* at what the ant is all about? Like these *Atta cephalotes*— one of the fifteen thousand different species inhabiting our planet. This one cultivates crops of fungus for food. Others herd aphids, just as man herds cattle. And what about the warriors, the builders of bridges, roads, tunnels.... *Frightening,* isn't it?"

"About as frightening as The Crater Lake Monster, I bet," says Sheldon. He helps their father set up the lawn chairs. "Your movie choices blow, bro." He does a double take as some girls walk by. *"Hellowe honies,"* he says.

"They have a sophisticated communication system," says the narrator. "Specific messages are transmitted from one ant to another through the use of a chemical substance called *pheromones.* It causes an obligatory response. Did you hear that? *Obligatory."*

"I'd like to *oblige* her," says Sheldon.

BECAUSE THE MOVIE gets off to a slow start, the Kid walks to the playground at the base of the screen—but pauses before stepping onto the sand. The swing set seems smaller than the last time they were here. He supposes this shouldn't surprise him; it has been awhile since they last came to the drive-in, and he has gained several inches, almost entirely in the legs, so that he feels awkward and gangly and tends to slouch. A single girl is there, seated in the swing farthest to the edge. Stringy red hair hangs in her eyes and at the sides of her face, like his. He meets her gaze briefly then sits in the swing furthest from her. He feels silly sitting in the swing, immature, but he also feels dirty—realizes he is dirty, that he has not thought to bathe or to put on clean

158

clothes; that he is still wearing the wide-bottomed jeans from earlier in the day, the ones with enormous holes in the knees, and that he is wearing his tatty green shirt also, the one with the pale yellow horizontal stripes. Neither one of them makes any move to swing; both stir their sneakers listlessly in the sand. The freeway drones somewhere in the distance.

"Come on, you know what it's all about, baby, come on…."

He cranes his neck to look at the screen, sees a man and woman struggling on the beach, their hair being tossed by a sea wind, waves crashing against the breakers.

"Let me go *you son of a bitch!*"

"*Relax,* relax…."

He looks at the girl in the swing. She's looking up at the screen, face painted in its greenish half-light, mouth hanging open. He looks back at the screen.

"That's it," the man says quietly. He begins unbuttoning her blouse.

"*Okay,*" she whispers.

"I just want to get to know ya, that's all."

"*Okay.*"

159

The man cups his hands around the woman's breasts, which strain against her bra. She hangs her head back, sighs. The sighs produce a strange reaction in the Kid, a tightening in his groin, something he has felt before but never in association with anything, just feeling good. For the first time he notices that the screen has a texture, that it's not actually flat but grooved, corrugated, like the metal walls of the lot. He looks at the girl, who glances at him briefly.

"Now just take it easy. That's it. You're gonna be a good—"

He is wondering what the girl is thinking when the woman on the screen knees the man in the groin, causing him to double over, gasping and holding his crotch. The Kid looks at the girl but she is gone. Her swing rocks back and forth, chains rattling.

He scans the parking lot for her but sees only the piercing white light of the projector's beam and the glow of the concessions shack, the ghostly gray speaker stands, the darkened automobiles. It occurs to him quite suddenly that he has no idea where the Camino is parked, that he was paying virtually no attention on his way to the playground. He jolts out of the swing and begins

160

walking toward the cars, his shoes slipping in the sand, tripping over one of the railroad ties that box the sand in. He turns this way and that as he walks through the lot, wandering between cars, stepping between speaker stands. The faces of strangers stare out at him everywhere, muted by car windows, softly lit by console lights, by the cherries of cigarettes. When at last he locates the Camino it is only because it is parked backward and he can discern the silhouettes of his family; they are seated in their lawn chairs in its bed; *and* because the projector's beam has set fire to the divots in the windshield, one of which has become a crack and spread—just as his mother said it would—so that it runs half the length of the glass. So that it splits, branching, into new cracks.

THOUGH *THE GIANT SPIDER INVASION* tries to be comical (it's a bust as a *giant monsters on the attack* movie, there being only one giant spider, not an army as suggested by the title and poster, and this only a Volkswagen Beetle with legs welded onto it and its chassis covered in fake fur), it's the horrific parts that form a knot in the Kid's gut. His mother is not happy either, disapproving—as she disapproved of *Empire of the Ants*—of the sexual content and violence. She is particularly offended by a scene in which a teenage girl in a push-up top responds to a libidinous suggestion by her mother's hillbilly boyfriend that she "ain't no child no more" by waving her breasts back and forth, giggling, "Yeah, now I'm 35-24-35!"

His father doesn't seem to mind too much though, and Sheldon is *loving* it, especially when the same girl, wrapped in a towel and with wet hair, is startled by her cousin, "Larry"—who causes her to drop the towel, revealing buoyant, pale breasts and nipples the color of acorns. It is not lost on the Kid that each time something like this happens the camera zooms up on the body parts. What compels him so much about the towel scene is the suggestion of something dark beneath the girl's filmy panties, something he has never seen in any other movie.

Ultimately *The Giant Spider Invasion* relies upon explicit grossness to achieve its effect, as when the girl's alcoholic mother unknowingly blenders a tarantula with her Bloody Mary—and drinks it—or lingering on close-ups of policemen being sucked into the spider's oral cavity, which constricts and expands like a sphincter

162

until red-black blood comes gushing down their trousers—until their crying out to God and cursing and grunting and moaning becomes mere gurgling, mere suffocation.

They decide that they will not go to the concessions stand at intermission, in part because they have brought a cooler, but mostly because *The Giant Spider Invasion* is so disgusting, ending with the spider being superheated from within until its pink-purple eyes explode, causing milky pus to geyser everywhere, and globs of green slime to roll down its shanks like snot, within which the Kid thinks he sees the policemen's remains.

"How about some lasagna?" jokes his mother after, lifting the lid of the cooler, handing out Cokes.

"Oh yes, *please,*" says Sheldon. He looks at the Kid. *"Good* movie."

The Kid is thinking about lasagna, about tomato sauce dripping, ricotta cheese oozing. "You seemed to enjoy it enough," he says. He looks at all the people wandering to the snack bar and the lavatories—equilibrium off balance from sitting, shuffling like zombies. "So did Dad."

163

His father chuckles. "That last one was pretty rough, buddy. Wasn't it, Mary Lee?"

"Oh, yeah," she says. She leans back in her chair, holds her Coke in her lap with both hands. It is unusually hot, even for July; her brow is beaded with sweat. She picks up the newspaper and fans her face and neck. "Seems every movie we see now days is full of sex and violence and profanity. Even kid's movies. I liked that *King Kong,* though. And *Close Encounters."*

"Those were family movies," says Sheldon. "These weren't *even* that." He climbs out of the Camino's bed, leans against the fender. "And we're not kids anymore, Mom. Not even *the Albino String-bean."*

The Kid looks at him through his bangs.

"I'm going to wander around a bit," says his brother, looking back at him, then walks away.

They sit in silence, sipping their Cokes.

"I was here when they had that earthquake," says his father, legs outstretched, eyes rheumy. "The whole car went like this…" He gestures palm down, as though his hand were a boat on the waves.

164

THE KNOT IN HIS GUT does not go away during *The Food of the Gods.* It grows. He could not have planned a more perfect storm—horror piling upon horror until he himself hates the movies he has chosen, wonders what could be wrong with him that he wanted to see such things, what *has* gone wrong with him—as a boy, a student, a brother, the Kid.

Sheldon by contrast loves *The Food of the Gods;* he can see it in his brother's face. It does not hurt that the main character, Morgan, is a professional football player, or that his best friend and sidekick, Davis, is also a football player, or that their rapport is just like Sheldon and his friends'—large, strapping fellows, working hard and playing hard. When Morgan and Davis are not playing football they're hunting deer on horseback with rifles and dogs—somewhere in the Northwest wilds far from New York and L.A., where they actually live, respectively—where they waste no time drawing pictures or writing stories but wash their sports cars and lounge by pools; where beautiful women are drawn to them because they are men of action and wealth. They do not

165

hesitate or fear or brood, and they never work or play alone but always in a posse, a *team*.

But because the Kid has chosen the movie—not his brother—no one has been carried off the turf on the shoulder pads of their buddies. Sheldon does Westerns, war movies, sports dramas, white hats defeating black hats. The Kid does rockets, new worlds, the unknown, *Danse Macabres*. The movie will not end with a freeze-frame of Morgan giving the peace sign with both hands. Already a man has died horribly—stumbling through the bramble with a two-foot long yellow jacket on his back; crying out for his friends, his face swollen purple, the wasp's black legs hooked into his abdomen, stinger pumping, cellophane wings beating. Already an old man has been eaten alive by rats the size of wild boars—his blood hemorrhaging, his face white with terror, screaming, *"Oh God, oh God! Oh dear God! Lord, save me, save me!"*

The Kid asks his mother if he can have some money for a 7-Up—to settle his stomach. She opens her purse and hands him three dollars, says, "Next time *I'll* pick the movies."

166

He nods and swings his legs over the bed rail, begins walking toward the snack bar. There is a glint at the periphery of his vision as he passes the front of the car. He looks over his shoulder but keeps walking…it is a stream of transmission fluid, glinting red-black beneath the orange sodium arc lights—winding away down the asphalt like blood.

THEY HAVE MOUNTED a speaker in the corner of the snack bar, near the ceiling, so that theatergoers can hear the movie as they wait in line. "I know all about delivering babies," says Mrs. Skinner, whose husband has been eaten alive by giant rats. "Living on a farm you get to know those things. Everything's going to be all right." She is talking to a young woman named Rita, who is about to go into labor. They are holed up in a cabin, waiting for the rats.

He weaves through the maze of metal handrails and waits in line, which consists mostly of older teenagers and some people in their forties. The fluorescent overheads cast everyone in a pale-yellow light; the floor is covered in sawdust and cigarette butts like the hog pens at the Interstate Fair. Everything smells of hot butter

167

and rank perfume and armpits and tobacco. He doesn't recall the first time he was allowed to go to the snack bar alone, but supposes it could not have been long ago. His stomach grumbles and his intestines shift audibly; he looks at the menu by the ceiling as the line moves forward, decides he'll get a hotdog as well as a 7-Up. He wipes the sweat from his forehead, grips the metal railing. His knees feel wobbly. A slight chill crawls over his skin.

The movie plays: "If I told how I felt right now you'd think I was crazy..." Lorna, the good-looking biologist. He knows it because of her clear voice and enunciation. "Tell me," says Morgan.

"I want you to make love to me."

He watches someone behind the counter scoop dregs from the popcorn machine, hears it begin popping fresh kernels, its glass sides shimmying.

"It is crazy, isn't it? At a time like this?"

"Listen, the first thing we'll do when we get back to the mainland is continue this conversation, okay?"

"That's just it. I don't think we'll ever get back."

He reaches the counter where he is met by a pretty girl with dark eyes and shiny black hair. He lays the bills on the counter and looks at the menu. The plastic letters swim in and out of focus. "I'll take a regular hotdog, and…" He rubs at his eyes, swipes at his hair "—and a medium 7-Up. Please."

"What?" She chews her gum.

"A 7-Up. Medium, please."

She begins punching the register's keys. "What else?"

"A hotdog. Regular."

"Two seventy-five." She takes the bills and slides him a quarter. He stares at her a moment before realizing she is waiting for him to get out of the way, that there are others behind him.

He gets out of the way, stands by the popping machine which rattles and shakes. He watches her through the glass, wonders what she looks like beneath her towel; if she has the type of breasts which strain against her bra or small pale ones with nipples the color of acorns. He wonders what kind of panties she wears, what texture, if they are thick like cotton or filmy like silk. He wonders what lies beneath—does she have a darkness, a demonic sublime, like the girl in *The Giant Spider Invasion?* Do all girls? Does the world?

169

"THEY'RE ATTACKING AGAIN, I need more shells."

He does not feel strong enough to walk back to the car and so sits on the grass in front of the projection booth. Morgan and the others are making their final stand against the giant rats, breaking out windows with the butts of their shotguns, pumping and firing into the horde, knocking the rats off the porch and the railings, sending them flying, causing them to scream and snarl, to regroup, to attack again and again. The Kid chews his hotdog as the scene shifts to the basement, where Lorna and Mrs. Skinner are acting as midwifes to Rita, who lies in the dark, rubbing her belly, listening to the blasts and the growling of the rats, listening to the wood splinter as they tear and gnaw at the cabin, as they claw at the planks and pull on the shingles. "How's it going?" Lorna asks Rita.

He finishes his hotdog and crumples its paper boat, takes a sip of 7-Up. He isn't sure if he feels better or not; he thinks perhaps not.

"I'm laying here thinking about what it's gonna be like when those rats get inside," says Rita.

"Morgan says we're going to be fine."

170

He lies back on the grass and stares up at the projector's beam.

"Do you believe that?" asks Rita. "You know, I used to think about dying a lot. Sort of lie there, in bed...at night...in the dark. I don't know. I guess I've always had a terrible fear of it."

"Rita, don't."

From this close he realizes that it is not one beam but many; he counts them, 5—6—7—rotating, full of blue-green smoke, as though colored smoke bombs have been lit nearby. He realizes that it is not in fact smoke but steam, issuing from a vent high on the wall, billowing and pluming. The beams are full of insects, gnats and mosquitoes and moths and stick-bugs, which beat their wings in the flickering light, circling aimlessly, chaotically. He hears cars on the freeway somewhere to the south, a constant whooshing, a gray-white noise.

"I could fantasize the most horrible death. You know, the most frightening. None of them come close to being eaten by rats. Funny thing is, now that it's happening...it doesn't really seem to matter."

Something kicks him in the pit of his stomach and he feels like he is going to ralph, is sure of it. Perhaps it can be avoided. Perhaps if he doesn't move, doesn't breathe, it will pass. "This too shall pass," his mother always says, and he hopes she's right, because *puking is the worst thing in the world.*

"What do you think our chances are?" asks Thomas, Rita's husband.

"Pretty good," says Morgan.

"Yeah, *like hell...*"

"Have it your way."

He is going to ralph—he is certain of it now. He climbs to his knees, sees Morgan filling jars with gunpowder and strips of cloth, preparing for the final onslaught. The Kid looks at the side of the building, remembers that the door to the men's room at the East Sprague is inside the concessions bar.

"Look, goddammit," says Thomas, "those rats are gonna bust in here and you're still fussing around with some *lousy jars!*"

"It's something to do," says Morgan.

"Something *to do?!*"

He struggles to his feet, holding his stomach, weaving back and forth. Right here on the grass or

172

halfway to the restroom? Squirting between his fingers or full-throttle ahead?

"That, my dear boy, is what life is all about. From the time you're born it's finding something to do while you're waiting to die, and you try like hell to prevent it. Now you get your ass in gear and get over there and put that strip in that gasoline jar and *move it!"*

He covers his mouth and hurries through the door, rushes toward the men's room—*hold the pickle, hold the relish, special orders don't upset us, all we ever ask is that you*—bursts into a stall and drops to his knees. He grips the toilet seat in both hands—*have it youuur way, at Burger King, have it youuur*—lets fly.

WHEN HE SWINGS OPEN the door of the men's room he sees Sheldon standing at the concessions counter, chatting up the girl with the dark eyes and shiny black hair. Sheldon looks at him as the door's hinges squeak. "There you are! Everyone was wondering what the hell happened to you."

The Kid just stands there, dazed. "I'm okay," he says.

173

His brother looks at the girl, hooks a thumb over his shoulder, laughs politely, insincerely. "That's my little bro."

"Hi there, Little Bro," says the girl.

The Kid looks from his brother to the girl. *Hi there, you little whore.* He steadies himself against a pinball machine. He feels a little better—a lot better, in fact—but isn't sure that he's out of the woods yet. He can hear the projector rattling in the room next to the lavatories.

"You know where the car's at, right?" says Sheldon. He's holding a cardboard tray piled with tinfoil-covered hamburgers.

"Yeah, of course." In fact he has paid no more attention than the first time.

"Okay," says Sheldon. He winks at the girl with the dark eyes, gives the counter a little pat.

The Kid watches him go. He supposes he is lucky to have a brother, though he misses the days when they were more alike, when they spent whole afternoons building model kits together, Sheldon's always coming out so perfect while his came out looking like the mix-matched Bondoed vehicles they often saw in Hillyard, gluey messes beyond hope.

174

"I think we ought to at least talk about it." — Thomas again, more from the projection room than the speaker on the wall.

"Pick up those jars of gasoline, Thomas."

The Kid stares at the door to the projection room, which hangs ajar. He walks toward it.

"You're gonna kill us…."

The rattling of the projector intensifies as he nears, going *tat-tat-tat*….

"And open the front door!"

He pauses outside the projection room, brilliant green-white light flickering through the door crack, painting his shirt and arms and hands. The *TAT-TATTING* of the projector is louder than he expected. A posted sign reads: NO SMOKING IN THIS AREA. He nudges the door enough to see partially into the room— feels a wave of heat wash over his face. Because of the angle he sees nothing complete, only the side of the projector which resembles a phaser cannon he saw on *Star Trek* once: a great, gunmetal gray thing, with cables coming out of it and lights along its side, and beneath those, huge horizontal film platters, grinding slowly, heavily, like the greased stone rollers in *The Ten*

175

Commandments—when Pharaoh's obelisk is risen in Cairo—and above all that, dryer hoses, only bigger, snaking up from the machine like tentacles, boring into the ceiling—itself made of stained wooden planks, like the sauna at the YMCA, to combat all the heat, he imagines. The sound of the projector and the sounds of the movie merge to create a cacophony of clicking, whirring machinery and discharging shotguns, of shattering glass and splintering wood, of the screams of men and women and rats killing and being killed.

He looks at the wall nearest him and sees a poster thumb-tacked to its grooved foam surface; it is the width of a magazine turned sideways, and is about two and a half feet-tall. It depicts a thin, fit woman wearing a derby hat and knee-high boots, but nothing else. She is seated on the hood of a car with her long legs elegantly splayed—like a spider's only white, hairless, smooth—knees bent so that the heels of her boots rest on the clean chromed bumper. She is smiling at him in a way he has never been smiled at before, chin down, a tumble of blonde hair covering one side of her face, spilling over a breast, flowing around an acorn-colored nipple. She has a hand placed on the hood of the car and another on her

176

groin, so that the tips of her fingers touch a fold-like opening, which gives and curls like pink flower petals, but which is surrounded by darkness and wild cruel brambles, and which she has parted slightly to reveal a red-black cavity, a fleshy knob, like the hole in the chest of someone having open-heart surgery; like the mouth of a cave or a window to another world.

VII | Drive-in of the Dead

HIS VIEW IS BLOCKED by someone's face—which fills the crack in the door, trains an eye upon him. He jolts away, staring dumbly, then bolts from the snack bar, shoving through the glass door with both hands, turning and wheeling on the boardwalk, looking for his brother. Surely he could not have gone far; surely he must still be visible, walking toward the Camino, his stupid white pants glowing, his feathered hair trailing, his clam-shell necklace glinting. He looks at the screen and sees poor Mrs. Skinner—who reminds him of his mother now that his mother wears earth-toned pant-suits and an Aqua-net scented beehive; now that she seems so passive and resigned and carries the leather-bound Bible

177

everywhere—in a death duel with one of the rats. The huge rat has crashed through the window of her kitchen and locked its jaws about her neck, is thrashing its head violently as she punches and struggles and kicks. She grabs hold of a meat cleaver and starts hacking the rat's face—but is knocked to the floor, shrieking, blathering, begging. "Oh, God—*oh, God!*" Until her windpipe is severed and blood gushes everywhere; her hands letting go, the cleaver clattering against the tiles—her eyes becoming black glass while blood spreads like spilled ink across the floor.

He begins trembling violently, turning this way and that, knowing he cannot find the Camino, knowing that if he did it would not make any difference, it would not stop the ground from rolling or the killer bees from coming or Skylab falling or Mt. Saint Helens from erupting. It would not stop the transmission from bleeding or the windshield from cracking. It would not stop the projector from burning out, from leaving them all in blackness, to shiver and die alone. It would not stop time—nothing could.

He is incoherent as he stumbles around to the side of the building, pauses against the wall. He looks at the screen even though he knows he shouldn't: sees Lorna the good-looking biologist holding her head—Lorna who has been so cool and determined and unbreakable, who also reminds him of his mother, his old mother, like the Unsinkable Molly Brown on the *Titanic;* the mother who waded into a cloud of bees and came out with four screaming kids; who gathered several more into the bed of the Camino and floored it to the hospital. Who saved Ricky's life; who *had* to—because *he* tripped over a cord. Because he hadn't been watching where he was going, never did. Because he could not see what was right in front of him, beneath his nose. *That* Lorna is holding her head, cowering just as he is, mewing, *"Oh, no, no, no…"* as the rats eat through the ceiling and wood splinters and glass showers; as Rita goes into labor, sweating, cursing, pushing in spite of everything.

HIS BROTHER IS INFURIATED that they have to leave early, before the film is even over—mutters something about how another family outing has been ruined by his baby brother, who *has* to be special. He wastes no time in trying to expose a nerve, suggesting the

179

movie is too mature for him, that he should be careful what he wishes for because he just might get it.

"It's nothing to do with the movie," insists the Kid, teeth chattering in spite of the comforter draped over his shoulders. He sits with his legs dangling over the tailgate, still trembling as though he were having an epileptic seizure. He has had to sit for fear of passing out; sitting, it turns out, will not do either—he cannot bear to touch the tailgate, much less the asphalt. Even the comforter does not comfort but weighs heavy upon his shoulders, smothering, suffocating, scratching his arms with coarse little hairs. The material world itself has become unreliable.

"Yeah, right," says Sheldon. Behind him, up on the screen, Lorna is telling Rita to "Push, push," as the baby is born. "You sure seemed all right before it started."

Had he? There hadn't been any *real* reason not to be; they were still on summer vacation, technically, and Mom was still allowing him to grow his hair, which he'd need in Junior High. There was the Booker thing, of course, and the math thing, and the thing with the tape recorder. There was the thing with the beehive and the Bible on the dash—but so what? What did these amount

180

to but temporary setbacks and phantasmagoria—things which could be fixed or figured, eventually? Everything had changed— nothing had changed. Mom was still Mom—though in an earth-toned pant-suit and an Aqua-net beehive. Dad was still Dad in his white cardigan sweater and his pleated Khakis and his greased hair—though he'd grown a mustache and thick sideburns—while Sheldon; well, Sheldon was Sheldon—polite, insincere, patronizing—the same old brother only masquerading as Leif Garret. And *The Food of the Gods,* about which he'd read so much, had come to town at last; and could now be viewed at drive-ins all across the country, which made for a lot of giant wasps swarming a lot of dumb football players.

"I'd say I was euphoric," says the Kid.

"So what the hell was the problem?" asks Sheldon as they pull out of the theater, everyone honking as their headlights sweep the screen. The Kid remains silent as they exit the gate—the tires of the Camino clanking over the 'no entry' spikes—peers behind the screen at the rusted iron girders, like the ribs of some giant carcass, and the scaffolding covered in pigeon shit. A wino has taken refuge using the girders to support his shelter—a

181

red-black blanket with tattered edges. The Kid doesn't know what the hell the problem was, exactly, but as they motor up the hill overlooking the drive-in he sees the place with fresh eyes, viewing it as a kind of graveyard, its speaker stands like tombstones and its cars like black, shiny coffins, waiting to be returned to the earth, and so also with the concessions stand, its painted wood mutating, fossilizing, and the neon lights, their gas and their filaments breaking down, becoming something else, while the gnats and mosquitoes and stick-bugs have it their way, multiplying and dividing out of control, as weeds push up through the cracks and the people who are but shadows bleed silently back into shadow. He doesn't know what the problem was, other than he'd had a sudden premonition that something terrible was going to happen—to the drive-in, to Spokane, to all the people (even the wino), to his mother and father and brother and himself. They were all going to die, *just go away.*

Eventually.

HE IS RUMMAGING through his shelves, looking for the decal set for his Concorde SST model, when his fingers snag a rack of tempera paints—spilling it to the

182

floor in a shower of colored tubes. He has tried to keep moving since they've gotten home, tried to still the shakes by organizing his *Famous Monsters of Filmland* issues by month, by arranging his Micronauts in little rows, like a military parade; by finding his SST. He is crouched by the shelves, picking up the kinked metal tubes, reading and sorting—bottle-green, oyster-white, chestnut-brown—his fingertips shaking, when he sees his mother, standing in his bedroom doorway. She is wearing his X-Ray glasses, which he recalls leaving in the bed of the Camino. He knows she is trying to be cute, to make him laugh, but he can't, not after ruining everyone's night.

He stands, brushing his pant legs. "Sorry about tonight…for picking those movies…and for freaking out like that."

She doesn't act as though she has heard him—only cocks her head, grinning. He sees that the ceiling light is reflected in the lenses of the toy glasses, realizes that for her the light has become the word 'X-RAY.' "Hold your hand up to the bulb," he says.

She does so, moving her hand back and forth, wiggling her fingers.

183

"It makes a halo around them," he says. "Makes the light bleed into your joints, so that your skin looks like bones, and the halo looks like skin. What do you think?"

She lowers her hand and looks at his wall paintings: superheroes and villains, the Milky Way, a mural based on Rudolph Zallinger's *The Age of Reptiles*—and Dagora-Carcinoma, his body hidden by clouds, his tentacles reaching.

"I think," she says, and stops. "I think…that you've been born into this mystery, just like the rest of us. That… it's a mystery so great…" she pauses, her face in shadow, "that men and women, especially parents, will do anything, anything, to deny it." She takes off the specs, smiles at him. "Just so that they and their children can get through the day." She folds the paper frames and holds them at her side. "The years. Look at you. I told you, 'You'll—'"

"Be taller than my brother. I know, Mom."

She enters his room and sits on the bed, pats the bedspread next to her. "Come here, sit."

He goes to the bed and sits.

"Give me your hand."

He gives her his hand.

184

"Close your eyes—keep them closed, no cheating."

She maneuvers his hand under her shirt, causing him to wince as his fingertips brush her flesh, which is startlingly warm. "Mom—"

"Shhh."

She guides his hand up her abdomen, sliding it smoothly over her skin until its palm rests partially on a rounded hump, which he determines to be the bottom of her left breast. "There," she says, almost whispering, and takes her hand from his wrist. "Hold it there." She folds his fingertips so that they rest upon a tiny lump, which gives softly beneath the pressure, and is no larger than a robin's egg. He can almost feel the blood racing beneath its surface as she breathes, her breast moving up and down.

She says: "You asked me once what a globular carcinoma was, remember?"

In his mind's eye he sees something red-black and saw-edged, with bitter teeth.

"And I told you it was probably one of your monsters—which of course you didn't believe, or partially believed, or chose to believe."

185

He imagines tentacles sprouting from the red-black thing, radiating out from its center, seeking purchase.

"But I knew what it was, because I had one inside me, or something like it. I found it the day your father brought home the El Camino. That one turned out to be benign, meaning harmless. This one isn't. Do you understand?"

He squeezes his eyes closed as the thing's tentacles split, multiplying, spreading throughout her breast, turning everything red-black.

"This one must be removed, the only question being should they take the whole breast, or just this lump?"

"They should take the whole—"

"Yes, that's what your father and brother think. But I have my own ideas. And I've decided they should take just this lump. Because my breast is part of me, and I'm a part of it; we've been through a lot together. So they can take Lumpy here and I will remain a whole woman, not a lopsided one like that hunchback in your Creature Feature—"

"Igor."

"Igor, exactly. Dr. Frankenstein's assistant. And then they will bombard the area with X-rays until the cancer is

186

all gone." She removes his hand gently, tells him to open his eyes. There are dark spots above her cheeks, fine wrinkles around her eyes. Yet her complexion is tan, plum, glowing. "So you see. I'm not going anywhere just yet. In fact, I'm not going anywhere period. I may be in a life and death struggle, but I'm not dying. I'm going to fight this. I'm going to beat it."

He stares at her, not blankly but without particular intent. It is as if some kind of autopilot has taken over. He isn't sure what he is feeling or if he is feeling anything. But some of her words have lodged in him, taken root—will stay there, he suspects, forever. *X-ray bombardment. Not going anywhere. Life and death struggle.*

"What if—"

"There is always *what if.* But there's no room for it—not in a life and death struggle. Not when it's underway. It's kill or be killed." She gets up, folds back the blankets. "You've got an appointment in the morning, at the principal's office. Go right to sleep. No TV." She turns on a lamp, switches off the main light. "And for heaven's sake, *no* horror movies."

187

He lies in the lamplight and stares at the wall, at Dagora-Carcinoma.

She pauses outside his room. "If you do well tomorrow you'll be allowed to advance, in spite of the math. Otherwise you'll be held back. That's the flat of it. That's how they explained it." Hinges creak as she grips the doorknob. "Remember. The dinosaurs couldn't adapt and that's why they became extinct."

Then she shuts the door—firmly, completely.

VIII | Dime-store Gazelle

WHEN HE OPENS THE DOOR to the principal's office he sees Booker right away, sitting half on the edge of the secretary's desk, smiling rakishly as he looks up, the conversation interrupted, the circuit closed. The Kid thinks he has never seen a smile vanish so quickly, so completely, as has Booker's. He walks toward the counter using baby steps as Booker ducks his head into the principal's office, his tanned, hairy hand gripping the doorframe.

"I'm here for my exam," says the Kid, feeling foolish because he doesn't even know what to call it, this

188

test of his abilities, this test of his truthfulness and character. Are you even human? they seem to be asking him. Do you belong here in our public school with our beloved *human* children? Or should you be farmed out somewhere else: the insane asylum, maybe, or the traveling carnie freak-show, with the rest of your kind?

"Mr. Spitzer," says the receptionist, not unpleasantly. She is pale, slim, with oblong eyes, a narrow face. He has seen her before but only through the glass, of which the top half of the wall facing the hallway is comprised. "Here is some paper—college ruled, is that okay?" He nods. "Here's some pencils. Tiroga Number Twos. 1, 2, 3—is that enough?" He nods. "There's a pencil sharpener in the room, on the far side of the cabinet." She tosses the hair out of her eyes, which swings, scintillating, like liquid gold. "Shall we?" He nods.

She escorts him into a back room the walls of which have upper halves made of glass, one facing the hallway and the other facing the principal's office. The room has light brown wood paneling and a single round table with three chairs, one of which she pulls out. Besides the cabinet on the wall and the pencil sharpener, there is only

189

a framed print of some daisies and an enormous IBM clock, which ticks audibly.

The wooden chair creaks as he settles into it and she orients the paper in front of him, the ends of her hair tickling his ears. "Break a leg," she says, and then exits, closing the door firmly, completely.

He squirms in the chair, the seat of which is hard as concrete. He looks into the principal's office, sees the secretary reseating herself, hair scintillating, and beyond her: Booker, who looks at him before mouthing something to the principal, who remains out of sight—then leaves the room. The big IBM clock ticks, its seconds hand swinging upon its fulcrum. He watches kids passing in the hallway, some of whom turn to look at him, most of whom do not. He picks up one of the pencils, rotating it between his thumb and index finger, liking how the smooth, painted, octagonal edges feel against his skin. He places its tip—which the secretary has sharpened to a fine point—against the paper, at the top of the page, feels the lead break a little as he writes, in large block letters, TWILIGHT FALLS ON THE WEST-END DRIVE-IN….

"MR. SPITZER? COME ON BACK."

He gets up from the hard, wooden chair the back of which faces the principal's office, goes in. The secretary—whose name is Miss Ashbury—wishes him good luck.

"Please, have a seat," says the principal.

He sits. The chair is a lot more comfortable than the previous one.

The principal riffles the pages in front of him—lifting his chin on occasion, peering through reading glasses. The Kid looks around the room; there are no partially glass walls here, only a large window looking out on the playground, which is empty. A long plaque on the principal's desk reads: ROLAND R. BLAIN, PRINCIPAL. Next to it is a microphone and a switchboard. There is also a big IBM clock, on the wall by the ceiling, ticking audibly. "You seem to have written us an entire short story," says the principal, "'Twilight Falls on the West-end Drive-in'... only to cross it out and replace it with a prose poem, or something like it. Why?"

"It's supposed to be all one piece, sir."

"What?"

191

"It's supposed to be all one piece. The pages of the first part, the short story, are crossed out with big S's—"

"Yes, I see that."

"—to show that the hero—"

"Who is *you;* you're using first-person—"

"Sure, I guess."

"You guess?" The principal reads from one of the pages: "'I stood my ground as Dagora-Carcinoma beheld us, His slit eye blossoming—like red-black rose petals—spewing forth tentacles from the center of the screen—tentacles that rose and fell almost gracefully—picking up cars as though they were Matchbox toys, shaking out the occupants who fell dancing and screaming to the asphalt, breaking like pottery, one after the other, until the asphalt, being pushed up everywhere by tentacles under the ground, changed color, and became a red-black sea which heaved and scintillated. But I ignored Him and thus He was blind to me, concentrating instead on the tentacles coming out of my own gut, like little cobras, grappling with them one by one, snapping their necks like dry twigs.' *That's* first-person."

"Yes, sir."

"So answer my question."

192

"Sir?"

"You've written a short story only to cross it out and replace it with something else. Why?"

"It's all one piece, sir. The S's are illustrations to show that the hero…the hero has been killing his fears one by one, killing cobras. And so has made himself immune to Dagora-Carcinoma."

The principal drums his fingers on the desk, stares at him with something like pity. "Do you even know what carcinoma means, kid?"

"It's a type of cancer, the kind my mother has."

The principal starts to speak, hesitates. "I see. And 'scintillate?'"

"It's what Miss Ashbury's hair does."

Blain looks past him at Miss Ashbury. The Kid cranes his neck, peeks around the doorjamb, knocks on the wood. Miss Ashbury looks up and smiles, tosses her hair.

"I see," says Blain. He looks down at the pages. "So this—Dagora-Carcinoma. That's a metaphor?"

The Kid has no idea what *metaphor* means. But it sounds right; he'll go with it. "Yes, sir."

193

"And you know what a metaphor is, right? A figure of speech where a term is transferred from the object it usually represents, to a symbolic one? Like, 'Life is like a ten-speed bicycle. Most of us have gears we never use?'"

"Yes, sir."

"And Dagora-Carcinoma is a metaphor for—sickness? Mortality itself? Time and death?"

"Yes, sir. All those things."

Blain takes off his reading glasses, slips the tip of a frame into his mouth. He looks out the window. The Kid follows his gaze to the empty playground and the cookie-cutter houses, the fenced-in yards, a wash of gray sky. Some boys peddle their BMX bicycles up the street, waving and gesturing to each other, their hair tossed by the wind. Blain appears altogether different without the reading glasses, younger, more alive. He looks at his watch. "Excuse me…" He swipes the glasses back on and peers at a schedule tacked to the wall, then picks up the microphone and presses a switch. "It's summer time and that mean's baseball fever—catch it. Registration forms are in my office. Thank you."

194

He hangs up the microphone. He sits up and exhales, squares his shoulders. He slides a sheet out from the others, examines it. "This poem, or whatever it is. 'Dime-store Gazelle.'" He looks at the Kid over his glasses. "Were you trying to tell us something, Mr. Spitzer?"

"Yes sir, I was."

Blain taps his finger on the desk. "Well, that explains that." The telephone rings in the other room. Miss Ashbury says: "Mrs. Kumpon, line one."

"Tell her to hold." The principal starts scribbling on the page—scratching and pecking furiously. "Mr. Spitzer, do you feel that this was a fair test of your abilities?"

"I do, sir."

"Do you feel that anything was gained from this experience? Anything learned?"

"Yes, sir."

"Which was?"

"That I can leap, sir. That I *have* leaped, now that I know the truth."

Blain looks at him over the glasses.

"About my mother, sir."

195

A final scratch, a final peck. The principal stuffs the pages into a manila file folder and hands it to him, then tosses the reading glasses onto his desk and rocks back in his chair, jauntily, almost, his hands clasped behind his head. "I used to teach writing at the college-level, you know. Years ago. I notice you used a second-person point of view in that poem, or whatever it is. Any questions about that?"

"I don't know, sir."

"What?"

"I don't know what that is, sir. I just liked the way it sounded."

BOOKER'S CLASS seems to go on forever, mostly because the Kid can concentrate on nothing after his teacher's "public apology"—which he senses his mother's hand in. One thing is certain; he knows Booker would not have apologized without being forced to— something about which thrills him, makes him feel powerful. But he is thrilled also that Jenny keeps glancing back at him, her new braces gleaming—that he has been redeemed in her eyes; and that the red-haired boy who liked his first story, Kevin, also keeps looking

196

to him, as though he were someone special; someone who should be courted, maybe, for the power he can bestow.

When the bell rings and everyone hurries from the class, the Kid lingers just outside the doors to the wing, watching for Booker through the pollen-dusted glass, gripping his story and poem in both hands. He is debating whether to give the poem to Booker; for it is true that he was trying to tell them something when he wrote it. He was saying: You should not have underestimated me. He was saying: You may have your fun with me but only if I allow it or am unsure of the stakes. He was saying: Now that I know it's life and death I will kill you—kill all of you—before you are able to kill me.

He waits until Mr. Booker emerges but decides against handing him the poem. He doesn't need to— Booker happens to look right at him. It is a freak accident but it serves his purpose: Eye contact—on equal footing, neutral ground. To cement his victory, close the circuit. You will blink before I do, the Kid is saying. And Booker does, his dark eyes batting, after which the teacher turns and walks up the hall—where Principal

197

Blain greets him, throwing an arm about his shoulder, smiling awkwardly, guiding him into his office.

The Kid looks down at his poem and reads it again; as though it were a prayer, an incantation:

You work with what you have. What you are given. What you can find. If it's The Giant Spider Invasion not Dickens well then that's what you have. Daydreaming through your geometry classes may not be such a bad thing. You miss some numbers but you gain Grendel, because you like monsters. You miss more numbers but you gain a black monolith. Because you gain a black monolith you gain a cool shadow. The shadow gives relief. You study the bones. You study the white between words, where little white beings live. They have pointy heads, pointy scowls. You show them to Your Bully. He is confused, enraged. Allies. He doesn't bully you again. He crosses to the opposite side of the hall when you pass. One day, during recess, he asks earnestly if he too might see the little beings. You laugh until your sides ache. Then you tell him he has a booger in his nose. When the bell rings, you watch him slouch off to football practice. Your story receives the highest mark in English, and the

198

teacher reads it aloud. When she asks what a certain word means, you tell her it's made up, that it means, "Window." She smiles sweetly, wanly. A Patron. You run home to your drawings, shoving through bus lines, blowing past walkers. You cannot walk because you have not paid attention. Because you have not paid attention you cannot be weighted. Because you cannot be waited you leap. The bones become weapons. The weapons become words. The words become ideas. You leap and leap, you and your allies. Fraud! Cry the walkers. Witchcraft!

"Come on, Wayne! Let's walk together!" —Jenny. Jenny and Kevin, the red-haired boy.

THEY WALK SHOULDER to shoulder along Broadway Avenue, Jenny in the middle, the boys pretending as though they are pinball bumpers, ping-ponging her back and forth. She giggles and shouts as she careens between them, braces glinting, pigtails bobbing. When they reach the intersection at University Road the boys punch the button to cross north while Jenny punches the button to continue west. Just before the light changes the Kid leans close and asks her if she likes him. It isn't until they are trotting in the opposite direction that she calls, "I like you *both!*"

Hearing this sends a thrill through him but also makes him wary. The thought that she might like Kevin too had never entered his mind.

Kevin hasn't yet seen *Star Wars* even though it has been the number-one movie in America for a year. Kevin explains that his father hasn't "vetted" it—checked it out to see if it's appropriate—which the Kid finds stunning, unbelievable. He tells Kevin that he should spend the night sometime; that his parents will take them to it no questions asked.

By the time they reach Kevin's the clouds have piled high and it has begun to rain. Kevin tells him that if he takes Sinto, past his own house and down the hill, he can cut through one of the yards and get home twice as fast. The Kid hesitates, gazing down the street. Thunder rumbles and ripples across the sky. The air smells of ozone. He is still deciding when Kevin strips off his windbreaker and hands it to him, says, "Get goin', man. Take Sinto."

The Kid just looks at him.

200

"Get goin,' man."

He takes the windbreaker and trots down Sinto—putting it on as he jogs, zipping it up. He swivels and waves. "What's a little lightning compared to Booker?" But Kevin has already gone in.

He runs down the hill.

He slaps his back pocket to make sure the pages are still there, rolled up like a diploma—a royal decree—his legal writ proving him fully human, fully divine. The sleeves of the windbreaker go *swish-swish* as he runs.

Part Three

I | Fireworks

THE LUMPECTOMY HAS GONE WELL. Her doctors believe with near certainty that they have gotten it all. That nothing has spread to the lymph nodes and she will make a full recovery. But she has a long, nauseous August ahead in which she will be bombarded with powerful X-rays, five days per week for five weeks, which could keep her incapacitated into September, and will probably cause her to become gravely ill and to lose her hair. His mother believes a celebration is in order before the follow-up treatments begin—a road trip, naturally. Sheldon chooses not to go, opting instead to join his friend John Morrison's family on a fishing trip.

She insists they go to Kelowna, British Columbia, to visit Bedrock City—a theme-park based upon The Flintstones, for the Kid; but the Kid doesn't enjoy it, having lost his taste for dinosaurs, or at least ones that look like Dino—colored purple or Day-Glo orange or sherbet-green—with frilly humps along their backs. Because they take the El Camino ("124,000 miles and still unstoppable," his father says more than once) they are forced to stop frequently to buy tranny fluid, especially on their way home, so that they find themselves pulling into a town called Oliver at twilight just as a professional firework display is starting— apparently in celebration of British Columbia Day.

He is amazed by the rockets; how they shoot so high, momentum upon momentum, heat upon heat—then burst, crackling, into a thousand little stars. He and his mother watch them out the passenger-side window, their faces parallel to each other, as his father maneuvers the Camino through an area of grassy knolls, then stops and backs up a slope—ratcheting the parking break so that they remain there, the rear of the car with its minor dent pointed at the sky, where the fireworks boom and blossom like an interstellar conflict only within the

206

earth's atmosphere. He helps his father set up the lawn-chairs so that the two fixed-back ones flank the long recliner, which his father insists his mother lay upon, "Like Cleopatra," says the Kid, which causes her to laugh heartily as she settles in.

His father goes to the cab of the car, returns with his mother's camera and a pair of binoculars.

"Try these," he says, handing him the binoculars.

His mother takes the camera. "Cleopatra accepts this homage, Marc Antony." She gestures grandiosely. "So many Marc Antony's, so little time...."

"There was only one Mark Antony," says the Kid.

"Tell that to Liz Taylor," she says, and laughs.

Since the lumpectomy she has become buoyant—poking fun at people she would never have poked fun at before and generally behaving as though she were seeing everyone in a new and ridiculous light. Not in a mean-spirited way, but just to have fun. So it comes as no surprise when—realizing they are not alone among the knolls—she leans toward his father and whispers, "Looks like we have some hipsters next door."

The Kid gazes across the elm-dark dunes, sees a psychedelic-painted van parked half-hidden amongst the trees. It has an awning made of what appears to be pink, fake fur attached to it, which reminds him of the shag carpeting in his half-brother Mick's perpetually smoky apartment. "Those are hippies," he says, leaning forward in his chair, rubbing the growing pains in his thighs and his calves.

"Those were hippies. But now the war's over and they've adapted." She winks at him and at his father. "Now they're just having fun. Still running wild but with a whole new set of pretenses."

He looks at the van through the binoculars, adjusts the focusing wheel. There are four or five "hipsters" beside it, reclining in their own lawn-chairs, passing some kind of vase. He watches a woman place the vase to her lips and strike a lighter, sucking while keeping the flame going so that the flame curves into a little bowl at the bottom and makes it glow. She sucks and sucks, cheeks indented, hair hanging. Finally she looks up and tilts her head back, appearing to hold her breath, and seems to notice him watching her. She has long, straight hair the color of goldenrod and is wearing blue eye makeup in which she has sprinkled glitter. A firework explodes above turning everything green and gold.

Everything about the woman screams 'adult;' not adult in the sense that his parents are adult, but adult in the sense of 'forbidden,' although she couldn't be much older than his half-brother, Mick, who is 26.

He works the focusing wheel furiously.

Her cheeks dimple as she seems to smile at him; then she exhales, as though blowing a kiss, making an 'O' with her lips—which are shiny with lip gloss—puffing softly, her eyes narrowed and glazed. The smoke turns to rings in the air, expanding and dissipating. For some reason he thinks of his X-ray glasses, which are neatly folded in the pocket of his shirt—his brother's shirt, actually—the one with the stiff collar and the lapels like garden trowels, which he has "borrowed." He takes them out and unfolds them, feeling their frames, now thin as felt, and slides them on.

"Look," says his mother, squeezing his arm. He looks, the binoculars hanging loosely in his hands—sees embers twirling slowly back to earth, dying. "They're always at their most beautiful when falling," she says, smiling at the sky. Her eyes shine as yet another burst goes off, painting her face white and blue and red.

"Fantastic," says his father, cupping his eyes out of habit. *"Faaantastic.* You watching this, buddy?"

The Kid nods, gazing at the fireworks, hearing both the people nearby and people far off celebrating, gasping as each new missile explodes—while each new firework, for him, because he is viewing them through the X-ray glasses, becomes multiples of the word X-RAY—which spiral and dash and rotate and sizzle, which lance into space and open like umbrellas; which burn white-hot, flashing like warning signs, like drive-in projection beams, like yellow-jacket stings and pebbles against the windshield. And amidst all this, all the booms and snaps and concussions like thunderclaps, all the shrieking and exploding and frizzling—the howling and the hollering—he hears music.

Not the Music of the Spheres, which Fast Eddy talks about, but radio music, pop music: "Undercover Angel," by Alan O'Day; which is emanating from big speakers placed outside the van. He swipes off the X-Ray Spex and peers through the binoculars.

He sees that the woman who had been sucking on the vase is no longer in her chair; she has been lifted on the shoulders of a man, whose neck she straddles Indian-

210

style: her bare thighs supported by the man's hands, the threads of her cutoffs hanging. She glances at the Kid, or so it seems, maintaining eye-contact for a full breath before looking away—then crosses her arms and pulls her top over her head, dropping it to the grass, swinging her hair, grinning toothily, carnivorously, arching her spine so that the tips of her hair touch the small of her back. Everything turns white as a series of blasts rattles the windows, mellows to chromium-yellow, fizzles to green.

His mother gasps at the fireworks, "Look at that, sweetie...!" Her old Argus camera goes *click-click-click.*

He stares at the hipster woman.

She is magnificent beyond belief—the eerie green light painting her face, her hair, her breasts, her belly—while Alan O' Day sings about thunder and magic and dream. He feels it again—the tightening in his groin, the thundering of blood and fluid into *it.* The woman places her fingers between her lips and whistles, rocking upon the man's shoulders, rocking and being rocked. He hears someone saying his name, his mother, or even his father, or both. But it is as though they are a million miles away....

211

He hears the Camino fire up just as the grand finale is beginning, sees his father in the cab while his mother sits deathly straight in her lawn-chair, glaring beyond him at the woman—the hipster.

"We're leaving?" He glances at the van, where the woman has begun unzipping her cutoffs—diverts his eyes to the sky. "But we haven't even seen the whole show! The big finish…" He glances at the van—she's still unzipping—back to his mother, "We'll miss the entire clima—"

But his mother has raised her chin, arched an eyebrow. Which means it is time for him to stop talking.

HE HELPS HER WITH THE CHAIRS, doing most of the work himself, folding them up and securing them against the cab. When he looks toward the van again he sees that while the woman is still on the man's shoulders, she has not, in fact, completed the show, but only watches the fireworks, smiling breezily, self-satisfyingly.

It isn't until they have pulled down from the knoll and are well upon their way that he asks his mother, "Why would she act like that, that woman?"

212

"Because they wanted to get rid of us," she says. "So they could have that spot all to themselves. So they could go on getting high." She looks out the window thoughtfully. "And because she's an attractive, liberated, insecure young woman who will do almost anything for attention, for anyone."

He nods, thinking about it.

"She *would* do anything with anyone," says his father. "I knew girls like that in the 1950s. In Seattle. Mom's right."

"Yes," she says. "Mother's right."

But his mother is wrong. She would not do anything for anyone. She did it for *him.* Because he is so young and cute and has learned how to dress. Because he is wearing his brother's white shirt with the stiff collar and lapels like garden trowels. Because his platinum hair is turning gold and he's feathered it just like Shawn Cassidy. Because he has sloe-blue eyes, high cheeks, an upturned nose and a pert mouth. Because he has dark swooping brows like a vampire, and he draws and writes and is an artist; meaning he is sensitive, insightful; a ravaging lover—better even than Valentino—which she knew the instant their eyes met. Because he is the Kid

213

and there can be no other, certainly not those Neanderthals with their scraggly beards and shaggy legs with whom she was faking everything; whom she was using, surely, just for a free ride to the British Columbia Day firework display.

HE HAS MET A GIRL. Her name is Tilly. He meets her the second semester of 7th grade at a pep rally at North Pines Junior High. He first sees her as she is performing "The Entertainer" with the North Pines Cubettes—a group of about 30 girls who march and kick and swing their arms like cheerleaders, but are not, and so seem to the Kid and the Two Ks, Kevin, whom he met at Broadway Elementary, and Ken, whom he's met at North Pines, more attainable. She is not nearly the most beautiful girl in the line-up—he would have mistaken her for a boy were it not for her bare legs and compact abdomen and the slightest suggestion of breasts—but she is the cutest, being petite, elfin, and having short hair for a girl, shorter than most boys, including himself: chestnut brown and apparently unspoiled by anything, except a comb.

She and a friend appear in the entrance to the gymnasium shortly after their routine, having changed from uniforms into their personal clothing, then climb into the bleachers just four rows behind them. They do this from the side rather than the front. The Kid and the Two Ks try to act nonchalant as Mr. O'Dell, the Principal, takes to the stage, begins talking about spirit and achievement and all the usual clichés, as though he were President Nixon addressing Expo '74.

A wadded-up candy wrapper skips across the Kid's shoulder and bounces onto the polished wooden floor. He looks at the girls, for there is no one at this end of the bleachers but them. The girls stare straight ahead, as though Mr. O'Dell's speech were the most interesting thing in the world. When a second ball of wrapper bounces off his head he turns and looks again, but this time he sees the brown-haired girl struggling not to smile, her brown eyes glinting as his mother's so often do, chortling and laughing without any words.

He tries to huddle with the Two Ks, who are seated to his right, asking how he should respond, what should he do? But they are of no help at all, having had no candy wrappers thrown at them, and only want to know

215

if it is one doing the throwing or both, and if it is one then which—so they can compete for whoever is not doing the throwing, he presumes; because when he doesn't answer, they become suddenly sullen and distracted, facing forward again, as though Mr. Odell's speech were the most interesting thing in the world.

Yet a third ball of wrapper misses him entirely—passing on his left side so that it remains clear only he has been selected—and he turns to see that the brown-haired girl has lain her coat on the third bleacher from them, easily within reach. He sprawls across the bleachers and snatches it toward him by its sleeve, the brown-haired girl protesting, eyes laughing, as he puts it on and zips it all the way up—clasping its collar, rocking his shoulders, as though he were freezing and the coat has given him warmth, security, fuzzy feelings, everything.

"Hey!" she says. "Now give that back!"

Her voice is just what he would have expected: petite, compact, smartly-proportioned—yet there is the faintest lisp, because she has a small gap in the middle of her front upper teeth, which along with her finely-cut mouth and small chin and pert nose makes him think of

something Fast Eddy used to talk about: *Lines of Grace.*
The Necessary Imperfection.

He hams it up for a few moments longer before
taking the coat off and extending it toward her—then
drops it and pushes it through the bleachers.

II | Kiss

"HEY!" SHE SHOUTS AGAIN, her eyes no longer
smiling. "What did you do that for?"

But he has no idea what he did that for—only that he
wants to keep the circuit open, the current flowing, but
has no words, and so has settled for this, this
provocation. "My grandmother bought me that coat," she
says, "It's the only one I have. How could you do such a
thing? That was mean. It was worse than mean. It was
cruel. Do you have any animals? Because if you do I bet
that you're mean to them as well. What's your name,
anyway?"

"Wayne."

"Wayne." She glances at her friend and then back to
him. "Wayne what?"

"Spitzer."

217

She nods, thinking. "Okay, I'm Tilly, but that was mean!"

He stares at her, unsure what to do next. "Well maybe I'm just a mean boy," he says, and faces forward, as though Mr. Odell's speech were the most interesting thing in the world.

At last she says, "Would you go down and get it for me, please?"

He turns around and stares at her.

"Please, Wayne?"

He likes hearing her say his name, how she stresses 'please.' How she pleads with him, playing her part, and submits to him of her own free will. She has invited him into a ritual by throwing the wadded candy wrappers and he has accepted the invitation by taking her coat and doing something unexpected, something with a taint of imperfection, a *Demonic Sublime.* He believes he has acted correctly, entertainingly, with the right dash of grit, but cannot be certain. What he is certain of is that he likes her—this girl with the small, round shoulders and pale collarbone, with the tiny gold crucifix hanging around her neck—likes her and believes he can have her, if only he plays his part, if only he's faithful to the ritual and its demands.

"Wayne, please?"

He leaps from the bleachers and ducks underneath, finds her coat lying crumpled on the varnished floor; a floor so buffed and polished it may be cleaner than the coat itself. He scoops up the coat and hands it to her through the slats, watching in a shaft of light as she takes it gently and puts it on, clasping its collar, rocking her shoulders—smiling down at him gap-toothed as though he has just given her everything.

HE LIKES GIVING HER EVERYTHING, comes to define himself and his relationship to her by it, and is able to do it without a care because his parents' company, Farwest Painting, has won the bid for the entire Spokane Public School System, a system which, over the next several years, will be knocking down old schools and replacing them with new schools; schools sleek and slanted like the Spokane Opera House—formerly the Washington State Pavilion—that will look like SST hangers, moon bases, the Future. His father has shown him the plans.

219

He can give her everything because he has become, practically overnight, a prince among his peers—not just the Kid but the Rich Kid—whose parents seem to pick him up in a different vehicle each day: sometimes the Camino, whose dent has not been fixed (nor its transmission or windshield), sometimes one of two new work trucks, other times a brand-new Lincoln-Continental LTD which looks exactly like his Uncle Shane's, only white.

Their feelings for each other intensify quickly because there are no boundaries or limitations to govern them, in part because she is the latchkey child of a single, working mother (and so can come and go relatively free), and also because his own parents are so busy; working but working for themselves, so that they are not just 'making rent' like Tilly's mother but really profiting, some of which trickles down to him; so that he and Tilly have time and money to do whatever they like, which consists mostly of being dropped off at 'G' or 'PG'-rated movies—*The Muppet Movie* or *Every Which Way But Loose* or *Battlestar Galactica...in Sensurround!*—where they sit high in the balcony (if there is one) and hold hands.

220

That remains the extent of their intimacy until the last day of school on June 4th, 1979, when they duck into a corner by the school's front doors—partly to say goodbye (he is going on a trip to Southern California with his family; she is staying after school for drill team practice), but really to perform the next rite of the ritual, which involves him sliding a ring onto her finger which he has fashioned from a dollar bill by folding and re-folding it the way Fast Eddy has instructed, and asking her if she wants to go steady.

"We've been going steady since I beaned you with a candy wrapper," she says, and laughs. "Since you said that maybe you were just a mean boy but then handed me my coat." She tilts her head, her pupils darting back and forth, lays a hand on his shoulder. "You should kiss me now, Wayne."

He swallows and inches forward, trembling a little, takes her small, round shoulders in his hands.

"Don't be afraid," she whispers.

He isn't afraid, not really, just excited, because despite his obsessions and manias and self-absorbed talk, he suspects that this is the one true thing—the one thing worth doing, the only thing that really matters. He is not afraid because she has invited him and because it all feels so familiar, she feels so familiar, as though they have always known each other and always will, as though Life were somehow a sphere and not a line. He pulls her toward him, tilting his head opposite her own, leans in so that their lips barely touch. Her breath smells of Lemon Drops and licorice and chewing gum. A car honks outside the doors, which he recognizes as the El Camino.

They part a little and look at each other. Her eyes are shiny, playful—brown as tea. Her cheeks are alive with blood. She lays her other hand upon his shoulder, runs them both up the sides of his neck, into his hair. The Camino honks again. Seven taps, *Shave and a Hair-cut— Two bits.*

"Don't forget me, please?" The lisp again. The gap in the teeth.

He traces her eyebrows with his fingertips, glides them down her temples and around her ears until her face is cupped in his palms. "I love you, Tilly Marie."

He kisses her, pecking once, twice, then exits through the double doors, where his parents are waiting in the El Camino—now pulling a travel trailer—in the

222

bed of which are two massive dogs the same breed as Lassie, forepaws on the fender, tongues wagging.

"Rusty and Ginger," says his mother, eyes tittering at his reaction. "They're coming with us to California. And when we get back..." She holds a hand to the rear window, which the dogs lick and smear with saliva. "We're going to breed collies."

HE PLAYS THE KISS OVER AND OVER in his mind, re-enacting it, improving upon it, all the way to Southern California, listening to the Camino's Motorola, to "Kiss You All Over" by Exile and "Sharing the Night Together" by Dr. Hook, to "How Deep Is Your Love" by the Bee Gees and "Undercover Angel" by Alan O'Day, watching rock striations change from a chalk-gray to clay-tablet red, watching horsehead pumps see-saw and refinery towers vent fiery plumes, watching desert palms pass beside and overhead, until, while at a rest stop just outside Santa Barbara, Sheldon pulls up to them in his black 1970 Firebird—smiling rakishly, his thick, wavy hair strewn by the wind, his friend John Morrison doing likewise.

223

"It's a good thing that trailer is as bright white as the Camino," says Sheldon, "or we would have lost you in San Francisco."

And then he laughs, good-naturedly, insincerely. Their mother is not amused.

The resulting argument, while heated, blows over fairly quickly, the obvious issue being that while Sheldon behaves as if he is 18 he is still in fact only 16, and should never have dreamed of driving over 700 miles without their parents' permission, should not have lied to them about going camping with John Morrison's father rather than coming with them on the trip—because he was "too old for Disneyland or whatever other diptard adventures" they had in mind, which he said would only revolve around the Kid, anyway, *the Albino String-bean,* which is how he has always referred to him when he was angry, or poking fun at him, or otherwise just ruing the day his baby brother spoiled what had once been a perfectly acceptable nuclear family.

Thus they roll into Hollywood in a kind of family motorcade: the El Camino out front with its bug-splashed grill and travel trailer which rocks and sways—the Kid in the bed of the car with the two collies, both of whom are

224

big enough to stand with their forepaws on the roof, flanking him, so that their long noses part the air and their tongues loll from the sides of their mouths, which the Kid imitates as they rock and roll down Van Nuys Boulevard—their Washington plates gleaming and the Camino's front license frame advertising SPOKANE CHEVROLET—"Like the Beverly Hillbillies," his mother says later, laughing...and a waxed and buffed Firebird; the Firebird Sheldon found languishing in a field just three blocks from their house, with its burnt-gold exterior fading in the sun and its tires so bald so that the steel belts were showing—and bought with their father's help, restoring the car to its former glory and then some, adding front and rear spoilers, chromed rims, wide tires, a new paintjob.

They drive everywhere (agreeing to meet at Hollywood and Vine at 8 pm should the cars get separated), past Capitol Records and the ABC Television Building, past Mel's Drive-in and Pink's Hot Dogs, past Mann's Chinese Theater and the Hollywood Walk of Fame, going, stopping, going again, bumper to bumper in a river of blue and gold license plates—everything steaming, smoking, flashing—the Kid staring at the

225

silhouetted skyscrapers, ghost-black in the orange haze, and at the black people, at the Asians and Hispanics and burnt-bronze Caucasians, who swarm through the intersections and along the sidewalks, some of which are broken and split apart, their sections bridged with boards—the result of recent earthquakes, the Kid imagines, or even lava domes—who clomp over the wooden planks carelessly, not even glancing beneath, although there could be anything down there, simmering hot springs, red-black rivers of molten rock, bubbling tar pits.

It isn't until twilight settles that his parents begin to search for lodging, driving easterly on tangles of freeway, entering and exiting tunnels illuminated only by banks of green lights and the lamps of automobiles, settling at last on a KOA Campground in San Bernardino, which they book for two days because it has three available and contiguous slots (two for the cars and one for the trailer) and a pool.

He begs relentlessly to make a long-distance phone call, to which his mother consents, but only if he keeps it short. "No three-hour conversations with Tilly while we're away," she says as she folds open the doors to the phone booth. She dials the number for him, billing the call to their home phone, and heads for the pool. "Things are getting too clingy between you two, I think..."

He closes the glass doors slowly, quietly, listening to Tilly's phone ringing, watching his mother vanish in the gloaming, wondering what she would think if she knew about the four-hour conversations—the ones they have after the three-hour conversations—the ones they have in their beds—in secret—beneath the sheets, cradling telephone receivers—

Someone picks up the phone.

"Hell-hello?" he says.

"Wayne!" shouts Tilly, and shuffles the phone. "Oh my God, mother, *it's Wayne!*"

"Hallelujah," says her mother from the background.

"You have got to tell me about it," says Tilly, breathlessly, "the whole thing, every detail."

And so he does, telling her about Klamath Falls, the tallest waterfall he has ever seen, and the life-size Paul Bunyan at Trees of Mystery in the Redwood Forest, and Babe, the Blue Ox, and the tree that you can drive a car though but that they couldn't because of the travel trailer, and the tyrannosaur, also life-size, standing sentinel in

227

the moonlight outside Prehistoric Gardens in Port Orford, and about San Francisco and the Golden Gate Bridge and the skyscrapers that do more than scrape the sky but punch right through it, vanishing into the clouds, and everything in L.A., the HOLLYWOOD sign and the Homes of the Stars and Richard Nixon's house in San Clemente, with its steeply climbing drive and concertina-wired fence and guard shack at the bottom of the hill. He tells her and tells her until his mother pokes her head through the door and draws a finger across her neck, and he says he has to go but to remember what he told her just before he left, to which she responds, "I'll never forget, Wayne. Never, ever. Call me again as soon as you can, *please?"*

"I'll call you tomorrow, promise."

"He's gonna call me again tomorrow," she tells her mother. And to him: "Have fun, okay?"

"You too, Tilly. Goodbye…"

"Goodbye, Wayne!"

And he hangs up—but not before hearing her mother repeat, *"Hallelujah."*

228

III | Magic Kingdoms

THEY HEAD OUT TO UNIVERSAL STUDIOS the next morning after his father unhitches the Camino from the travel trailer. Sheldon and John opt to stay at the campground, ostensibly to look after the dogs but really, the Kid knows, to hang out by the pool and hit on girls. After being admitted to Universal they board a tram which consists of several passenger cars linked together, all of which have canvas roofs with crenulated skirting that remind him of the awnings at Kentucky Fried Chicken only colored blue and white. Although he is primarily thinking about Tilly he is floored when the tram pauses on a bridge overlooking a swampy, boggy waterway, knowing even before the tour guide announces it that he is looking at the Black Lagoon itself. The guide goes on to describe how the waterway is entirely man-made and lists some of the many other movies filmed in part along its banks and upon its waters, but the Kid just stares at the lagoon's glistening surface, as if he were seeing behind Oz's curtain itself, disappointed but thrilled by the banality of it, by the fact

229

that it is mere water same as anywhere else, even Spokane.

The tram continues along, slowing and pausing for each attraction…for the parting of the Red Sea from *The Ten Commandments*—a Red Sea about the size of the public pool he used to go to in the summer—the secret mechanics of which he cannot see but thinks he can hear, and into whose emptied ocean bed the tram clatters, down and out again, pausing on the opposite side so that the passengers can watch the waters rejoin, as if drowning Pharaoh's armies…for views of Universal's many working soundstages, which look like aircraft hangars, one of which was used for ABC's *Kolchak: The Night Stalker,* says the guide…for a re-enactment of the earthquake from Universal's *Earthquake…in Sensurround!*—during which windows shatter and water mains burst and street lights fall to within feet of the tram before stopping suddenly, held fast by guide wires…for an attack by 'Bruce,' the great white shark from *Jaws,* which begins with a fishing boat being broken in half by something just beneath the surface of the pool—spilling an automatronic man into the water which bubbles and froths and geysers, turning blood red, causing everyone

230

to scream and to laugh and to sigh with relief—at which exact moment Bruce the Shark lunges at them from the depths, rising and falling along the length of the tram so that everyone gets their chance to be lunged at…for an abduction by cylons from *Battlestar Galactica,* in which the tram is driven into the bay of a landed spacecraft where the show's hero, Apollo—played by someone other than the actual actor—appears, and engages in a pitched laser battle with the cylons—their beams flashing and glowing and crisscrossing in the smoke…for a trip through the cylindrical glass tunnel from a 2-part episode of *The Six Million Dollar Man* in which Steve Austin meets a bionic Bigfoot constructed by aliens—a tunnel which rotates around them as they pass, spinning faster and faster as the tram picks up speed and the cylinder narrows so that its glass sides close all around and become a dizzying, rumbling blur…for a dramatic rockslide in which boulders the size of Volkswagens bounce and crash down a craggy incline, making much noise and dust—like what would happen if Mount Saint Helens erupted, he supposes—only these boulders never hit them but vanish harmlessly into some kind of gutter—to be returned to the top so they can bounce and

231

crash down all over again, he figures, like in a bowling alley.

The tour ends when they disembark the tram for a walking tour of Lucille Ball's wardrobe, which his mother has been looking forward to immensely, but which doesn't interest the Kid. This changes when they enter a walk-in closet which is long as a house, and begin moving down the racks of dresses and coats—each of which has a distinct aroma, and each of which, together, share a collective aroma, a hint of Lucy, something so faint and nebulous that he suspects it is only his imagination—until he notices long red hairs clinging to the garments.

It is unbelievable to him that something so significant could simply be left behind and forgotten. He glances at his mother, finds her seemingly staring at the same thing, her eyes full of wonder. For the first time in days he notices the smell of Aqua-net hairspray and the strands of hair clinging to her collar. Something about this makes him think of the black lagoon, and how water is the same thing there as it is in Spokane. But then a jet passes overhead which causes the lighting fixtures to

232

rattle and the window panes to shake. And he loses his thoughts in the rumble and roar.

THEY GO TO DISNEYLAND after leaving Universal, his parents joking about how crazy it is to attempt both in one day, delighting in their own audaciousness, rushing because it is already late afternoon. They start with Main Street U.S.A., which the Kid has no use for because it seems to him they already live on Main Street U.S.A., in Spokane (although Main Street there was never so idealic and colorful, not even during Expo '74). Things get better when they board the Disneyland & Santa Fe Railroad—the same steam-powered locomotive he has seen on TV, but pulling four Universal Studios-style rail cars—which takes them around the entirety of the park, past dioramas of the Grand Canyon and the Primeval World, red skies, dinosaurs, great wheels clattering over iron tracks, engine chugging. But they are rushing everything too fast: Immediately after debarking they move onto the Swiss Family Robinson's Tree House, which the Kid fancies himself living in with Tilly someday, after he has become rich like his Uncle Shane, but by writing books and making movies; then onto the

233

Jungle Cruise and the Haunted Mansion and the Pirates of the Caribbean, the latter of which he refuses to go on until the attendant assures him that it is a slow ride and not a rollercoaster.

And it isn't a rollercoaster, as it turns out, but just the sort of ride the Kid enjoys most, one which moves leisurely yet assuredly past sights the eyes can gorge upon, until he hears a rumbling ahead and around the corner, and the mock boat they are in begins to vibrate, as the roar of rushing water draws nearer and grows louder, as he hears the people in the boat ahead of them—which has vanished into the darkness—screaming, and sees a faint red-black glow spread like blood over the cavern wall, and grips his mother's hand as the nose of their boat drops, causing his stomach to lurch, and they plummet blindly into the moist, screaming blackness.

He glares at the attendant as they disembark, lagging behind his parents on purpose and passing close enough to read his nametag—"Brad"—wondering if the older teenager has any idea whom he has trifled with, and recalling a chapter from one of his science-fiction books, *Stalking the Nightmare* by Harlan Ellison, in which the author recounts a funny story about being fired from Disney for 'fucking with the Mouse'—thinking: One could get fired from Disney for fucking with the Kid, too. The Kid who defeated Mr. Booker and won the heart of Tilly Marie McBride.

"It's not nice to trick people, Brad," he says, pausing directly in front him, looking him in the eyes. "Especially when you don't even know their name or who they are."

The attendant just shrugs and takes a step back— allowing the next group of passengers through. "I know exactly who you are. You're some kid who's afraid of a little ride. And I'm the guy whose job it is to put people on that ride. You had fun, didn't you?" He waves at the departing passengers, including his parents. "Bye-bye, folks! Enjoy your visit to Disneyland!"

He is still smarting, perhaps, from being so unceremoniously dismissed, when they enter the section of the park called New Tomorrowland—which he loves so much that he forgets the exchange entirely. He especially likes the monorail which swings them around all the sections of the park combined and gives them excellent views of Space Mountain and Sleeping Beauty's Castle and the Matterhorn, which seem tiny and

235

insignificant when viewed from the bullet train's curved windows, something he finds inexplicable considering how gargantuan they appeared earlier, when he and his parents stood right at their bases, posing for pictures and eating snow cones.

They can only visit a handful of attractions in New Tomorrowland because his parents want to get back to check on Sheldon and the dogs and still have time to just ride around San Bernardino—which is fine with the Kid because he's eager to call Tilly from the blue and gray phone-booth by the lodge—so they settle on Mission to Mars, Adventure Thru Inner Space, Submarine Voyage and Autopia. None of them affect him quite like Autopia, where for the first time in his life he alone is belted into a half-sized automobile—an automobile resembling a blue Corvette Stingray—which, though secured to a track, is nonetheless under his control to speed up or slow down as he pleases, to cock his arm out the window, to envision a future in which he and Tilly might drive themselves to Los Angeles or New York or Alaska or Argentina.

It isn't until the sun is sinking and they are accelerating onto Interstate 5, the Kid seated in the

236

Camino's bed with his back against the cab and a sun-burnt arm on the fender, Disneyland but a crenulated silhouette against the hazy, primordial sky, that it comes to him: Sleeping Beauty's Castle and the Matterhorn are tiny, insignificant; they are smaller height-wise than most of the office towers in Spokane, in some cases by half, and the only reason they appear gigantic up close is that their designers have used forced perspective to give them the veneer of height, building each new layer more miniaturized than the last until it seems the structures could penetrate the sky. But in fact they might just as well be made of tinfoil, papier maché—light itself, like images on a screen—another trick.

"TILLY—IS THAT YOU? HELLO?"

"Hi, Wayne! Hold on..." The line shuffles and creaks, "My little sister keeps tangling the cord—I've got to unplug the receiver a sec..." Everything goes silent.

He waits as she untangles the cord, looking through the glass at the campground sign, KOA AT SAN BERNARDINO, at the giant black, yellow, and red logo, and at the hoary, peeling palms and utility poles, all of

237

which lean in the same direction like variants on a theme, like ripples in water or undulations in hair.

"There," she says, exhaling. "Tawny's been on the phone all day with Grandma—" She covers the receiver, "And because she's immature and can't sit still for five seconds…!" She un-cups it, "…the cord was twisted into a knot, and how. She and Mom are going to visit her tomorrow, in Deer Park."

"You're not going with them?"

He sees Sheldon walking toward the lodge with a tall, blonde girl. The girl is wearing cut-offs and a bikini top and seems horribly sunburned, as does his brother. He can't hear what they're saying but can see even from this distance that Sheldon is obliging her every lip movement with a lip movement of his own—smiling breezily, insincerely. The Kid imagines that Sheldon's girlfriend back in Spokane would be proud. Such fidelity.

"I want to be here when you call," she says. "It's bad enough that we don't get to see each other."

He swallows uncomfortably. "Two more weeks. It'll be over before we know it. Want to hear about Universal Studios and Disneyland?"

"Sure," she says. "I suppose."

238

"Well I suppose I'll tell you…" And he does, telling her about Mission to Mars and the pressurized seats which made it seem as though they were truly blasting off to Mars—about Adventure Thru Inner Space, in which they were 'shrunken' smaller and smaller until they orbited a single oxygen atom, which pulsated like a star, and around which electrons zipped and fluttered like insects, until an enormous human eye opened, blinking as though looking at them through a microscope—about the Submarine Voyage which ended with an attack by the giant squid from 20,000 Leagues Under the Sea—its beak snapping, orange tentacles slithering, shaking the sub like a toy—like Dagora-Carcinoma, whom he has told her about: shaking people from their automobiles and smashing them like pottery. He is about to tell her about Autopia when his mother appears outside the glass and draws a finger across her neck, whereupon he says he has to go but again tells her to remember what he said before they left, to which she doesn't respond right away, only breathes into the phone. He realizes there are railroad tracks next to the phonebooth and follows them with his gaze to where they vanish in the gloaming.

"Do you miss me?" she says quietly.

239

He blinks and swallows, stunned a little. "I miss you more than anything. I love you, Tilly."

"I love you too, Wayne. And I'm going crazy without you."

His mother raps on the glass.

"I gotta go. I'll call you tomorrow, before we leave L.A."

"Okay."

"Bye, Tilly." And he hangs up.

BECAUSE IT IS WARM AND CLEAR his mother allows him to sleep in the bed of the El Camino, where he climbs into his sleeping bag hoping to see the stars but sees only a reddish haze which he supposes is smog. Nor does he fall asleep right away but instead tosses and turns, not liking the idea of Tilly going crazy without him—preferring she be going crazy with him, right now, kissing him all over, as he wants to do to her. Nor does he like that he carried on so long about Disneyland, betraying his boyishness and basic immaturity. He resolves to remedy the situation during the next call, at which time he will talk only of them, of what they will do together when he gets home and where they will go.

240

Somewhere between dim wakefulness and dozing he thinks of the parting of the Red Sea at Universal, likening it again to their neighbor's swimming pool, remembering staring into it once after it had been drained, in the rain, so that it seemed much more than a box-shaped hole but rather something abstract and impossible, the walls of which were made of water; and thinking also of beams of light in fog and black shapes beneath surfaces, of earthquakes and avalanches and spinning ice tunnels—when he sleeps, he dreams of rumbling.

He is so eager to leave L.A. the next morning that he brings a tray full of hot coffees into the trailer (which smells of dogs) and nudges everyone awake, having risen just before daybreak and wandered the campground until the doors to the lodge opened at six. But his mother insists they visit the Movieland Wax Museum before leaving—having read about it in *Life Magazine*—attempting to pique his interest by saying, "I seem to recall a certain young man having an interest in *Star Trek.*"

"Yeah, when I was nine," he says—but seeing how this hurts her adds: "You seem to recall correctly. That'll be far-out, Mom."

241

And it is pretty far-out; especially when they round a corner near the end of the museum and see the bridge of the *U.S.S. Enterprise,* walls lit blue and turquoise and mauve, its control panels glowing and flashing and buzzing—while the show's theme plays too loud and the wax crew members pose rigidly, Kirk sitting straight-backed like a mummified Egyptian Pharaoh, Spock standing with his arms pressed against his sides so that his entire figure could have been hewn from the same slab of wax, Bones with his elbows bent at odd angles and his face a bloodless mask; Uhura the most lifeless of all, having no lines of grace, no demonic sublime, no necessary imperfection, only blank eyes and frozen hands, stiff legs, stiff hair. It is as though the cast members have died only to be embalmed poorly and positioned like trophies, so that the room feels stale, airless, as though time itself has pooled and grown stagnant.

The next display is better, less stiff, partially because it depicts characters doing rather than posing, and partially because it recalls for him his first kiss with Tilly only a week ago. The plaque states that it is a reproduction of the kiss between Hedy Lamarr and

Robert Taylor from the 1939 film *Lady of the Tropics,* and it seems to him superior in every way because it has lines of grace—grace in how Hedy's long fingers curl about Taylor's neck and gently fondle his wavy brown hair, in how her face seems so serene, so trusting and frank, and he supposes it has the necessary imperfection as well because Hedy's own hair is so straight and uniform and her chin is too sharp and small. But of a demonic sublime there is no indication, other than Taylor's hands being placed upon her hips instead of her shoulders, which suggests to him a pulling down and a lying back, a flattening out upon the tiger pelt which drapes the bed. And again he finds himself replaying the kiss with Tilly in his head, reenacting, revising, so that he pulls her against him and kisses her the way people in movies and on TV kiss, seriously, intently, like Captain James T. Kirk—the living one not the wax one—not knowing if Tilly means it but knowing he does. That he could no more forget her than he could forget his own mother. That he could never willingly let her go, and that if she were to let go of him he would never accept it, not until his very last breath; and even then he would have found a way to preserve them, to hang them in space—as

243

they are now and always shall be—young, beautiful, innocent; preserved in a display of wood and wax and drapery, together forever.

And then they are on their way back, the Camino's engine running roughly—"Just needs a tune-up," says his father, causing his mother to roll her eyes—down broad highways and beneath overpasses and past no less than three drive-in theaters (which must never go out of season in Southern California, the Kid realizes), all the way to San Bernardino.

Bang, bang, bang, like that.

IV | Werewolf

HE GETS STUNG BY A YELLOW JACKET while swimming a final time at the KOA—a yellow jacket he was aware of, having seen it perched on the railing a short time before, just sitting listlessly on the super-shined chrome as though dying slowly beneath the sun's brutal rays. It stings him when he puts a hand over it while climbing from the water, having forgotten about it while swimming, while wondering what Tilly looks like in her bathing suit and her birthday suit, too; while

244

wondering what he'll find beneath her towel, like the girl in *The Giant Spider Invasion,* when the time comes— lines of grace or a demonic sublime?

He makes a point not to show how badly it hurts as he grabs his towel and heads for the trailer, knowing the slightest vulnerability will draw the attention of Sheldon and John and their little summer lovers—having come to the conclusion that much of what gives Sheldon his power and charm is the using of him as a foil: I am big because my brother is small—and choosing to deny him that.

His mother puts some Calamine lotion on it in the trailer, which helps the burning a little, but because the wasp has stung him in the webbing between thumb and forefinger it continues to hurt and swell and to grow red, which fact he uses to guilt his mother into letting him call Tilly.

"I still think things are moving too fast between you two," she says, dialing. "You're not even fourteen years old."

He watches her dial; listens to her speak to the operator. "I will be in about two weeks."

245

"On July fifteenth, that's right." She hands him the receiver. "Which is more like three weeks." She exits the booth. "Keep it short, kiddo. We're ready to leave."

He slides the doors closed and listens to Tilly's phone ringing. There will be no repeat of the last time— no talk of Universal Studios or Disneyland or the Movieland Wax Museum. He will conduct himself like a young man and not a little boy. He will speak like someone who has won the love of the girl but knows the love of a girl must be maintained. He will speak like someone who is about to turn fourteen: who, within a year of that, will have a learning permit to drive an automobile—a real one, not a half-sized one like at Autopia (the El Camino, perhaps, with her wide tires and eight cylinders). Whose mind and body are changing— rapidly, unmistakably, formidably.

Tilly's phone rings and rings.

He watches as his father backs the Camino up to the trailer, begins maneuvering the ball of its hitch under the socket of the R.V., while Sheldon and John gesture and direct. Everything shimmers through the grimy glass and the heat. He wonders what they would do if the trailer

246

could not be connected—would they simply have to leave it behind, abandoned, forgotten?

The bee sting itches and burns against the receiver as Tilly's phone continues to ring—it has already rung maybe seven times—his pulse quickening as he realizes she is not going to answer. As he realizes for the first time the danger of having been apart for so long; of having been lost in wonderland while she went crazy without him.

A freight train blasts its horn somewhere up the tracks, two long bursts: *Mrawww...mrawww....*

He hangs up the receiver and runs a hand through his hair—holds a fist to his mouth; as Dad pulls the trailer from the stall and Sheldon backs out in his Firebird. He knows their itinerary: south to San Diego then northeast to Las Vegas, where they may or may not stop for the night, then on to southeastern Utah where his mother hopes to find the farm on which she spent her childhood.

The crossing signals sound as the freight train approaches, the bells clanging hard and clear, and he sees the locomotive's red and black front bearing down, sun glinting off its windows and wipers, oily smoke billowing.

247

Mraw...mrawww....

He circles within the phone booth, fist still held to his mouth, then snatches up the phonebook and rifles its pages, finding a map of Los Angeles and a map of the United States—the bee sting galling his hand, the heat causing sweat to run down his face.

A moment later the engine roars past, pistons pounding, air valves popping, filling the air with the sound of clanking iron, causing the glass to vibrate.

He reads the legend in the upper-left corner of the U.S.A. map—each centimeter equals 50 miles, which is about the number of miles they average per hour due to the weight of the trailer—taps his finger along the map in multiples of 50—calculating quickly, efficiently, having no trouble with the numbers at all—figures 100 miles to San Diego with a 2-hour drive; 250 miles to Las Vegas with a 5-hour drive; 300 miles to Natural Bridges National Monument—or wherever they're going in Utah—with a five and a half-hour drive—where they'll have to stop for the night, if they haven't stopped already, but where there may not even be a phone, as they'll be in the middle of the desert. For a total of twelve and a half hours on the road, not including time

248

spent driving around San Diego and Las Vegas, where they may stop but probably won't knowing his parents (who could drive to the moon and back without breaking a sweat), and who are probably in as much of a hurry to get home as he is, considering construction on the schools begins in late July.

He starts bouncing a little on the balls of his feet as the rail cars blur past, feeling like a boxer—hopped up on adrenaline, hungry to dial again, yet knowing he won't be able to hear anything yet. He tries to see what his family is doing on the other side of the tracks, terrified that they will be ready to go, that he will not have another chance to talk with Tilly. But because the train is right next to the phonebooth and the gaps between box cars too fleeting, he gets only snapshots, and these only of things: The El Camino. The Firebird. The travel trailer. At last the whooshing box cars give way to a series of flat cars, over which he can see everything: The El Camino, shining in the sun, his father at the wheel, just sitting there, it seems, gazing straight ahead. The Firebird, rocking forward and back, Sheldon clearly growing impatient, revving his engine so that the tailpipes of his car give vent to little plumes of smoke.

249

Their mother, worrying over something in the travel trailer, picking at something upon her hands and knees (dog hair, probably), oblivious to everything else, her pant-suited buttocks hanging out the door. It is like watching a slide show in fast-motion, the wheels of the train going *chit-chit, chit-chit, chit-chit.*

Then suddenly the tumult is over, the train's yellow and black caboose has passed—clacking and rumbling down the tracks. The passing of the train comes so unexpectedly that it takes a moment for him to realize that he still has time to—

He snatches up the receiver and dials the operator, places a long-distance call to Sally McBride, Tilly's mother, asking that it be billed to Gifford and Mary Lee Spitzer at 20630 W. Mission in Spokane, Washington. She connects the call and he exhales, hearing it ring, falls against the glass, yet fears she will not answer this time either—knows it somehow, in his heart. The crossing bells continue to ring incessantly.

She picks up on the third ring, says, "I'm so glad you called back, Wayne!"

"Tilly? How'd you—I didn't think—it just rang and rang..."

250

"I couldn't get to it fast enough. I was outside, on the back porch."

He glances at his family's vehicles, sees that the door of the trailer has been closed and its break lights are on, meaning the car is in gear, they are ready to roll. His mother is standing by the passenger's door and looking his way, her hand shielding her eyes. "Look, Tilly, I just wanted—"

"Tell Richie Rich he has absolutely nothing to worry about. There's a fox guarding his hen."

He freezes, knowing the voice but unable to place it. "Who's that?"

He hears steel grating against steel somewhere down the tracks.

Tilly laughs. "My god, you're terrible. That's your friend—Kenny. Turns out he lives right up the road."

"Kenny…Ken Goodman?"

"Yeah—well I call him Kenny. You *have* been gone too long when you can't recognize your friends' voices. Pretty soon you won't recognize mine."

The crossing bells ring and ring. He looks up to see that the train has ground to a complete stop. He presses the receiver tight against his ear—hears little popping

251

sounds, like firecrackers, only milder. She cups the receiver, "Stop that!"

"What is it? What's he doing?" *And why is he in your house?*

"Your friend is throwing snap-pops at me—stop that! Seriously." She giggles.

"Tilly, I—" *Why is he in her house?*

There is a sound like decompressing air and he looks up again: But the train is just sitting there, its yellow and black caboose gleaming. The heat of the sun and of diesel exhaust have filled the air with convection waves so that everything shimmers like water. He glances at his family's vehicles, sees his mother storming toward the phone booth and his father's door hanging open, his leg outstretched. Sheldon has already pulled from the lot— the Firebird hardly visible amidst all the backed-up traffic.

He grips the phone, sweat running from his hair and down his neck, glossing his palm, making the receiver slippery. "Tilly, I—why is Ken Goodman inside your house?"

Another *pop!* Another giggle. "Hold on..." She cups the receiver. "Stop Kenny, please. It's long distance.

Who knows when we'll get to talk again…" She un-cups the phone. "You there, Wayne?"

More snaps. More pops.

"Nothing to worry about, pal! Fox guarding the henhouse!"

There is a hard shuddering from the boxcars—a series of iron *ka-thumps!* which start far away and ripple closer. "Please, Kenny?" The gap in the teeth. The lisp.

"Wayne's the fox."

He makes eye contact with his mother, who is almost there. She is fuming, her brow taught, her eyes narrowed. *I was outside, on the back porch.*

The train begins moving again.

"Tilly, listen. The dollar ring. Do you have it?"

"Of course I have it. It's on my finger. What kind of—"

"Would you do me a favor, *please?*"

There is a great, shuddering, grating sound—a result of the train picking up speed—followed by the *ka-krunk* of its wheels passing over gaps between rails.

"I'd do anyth—"

253

"Take it off and give it to Kenny. Tell him to unfold it and buy himself a candy bar. Or just throw it into the grass."

"What?"

"Just take it off, okay? It apparently doesn't mean anything." He watches the yellow caboose as it begins shrinking, the windows of its cupola becoming indistinct, its railing and handholds blending back into the whole—into the horizon.

"What are you—"

"Take it off! We're done, it's over!"

His mother reaches for the doors—he jams his foot against the fold, locking them into place. "Just go on and play the slut with Kenny, all right? Tell him when I get back I'm gonna bust his teeth out. Okay? Could you do that?"

"That's not it at all! We're just friends—"

"Open this door!" says his mother, pushing on the panels, her face enraged.

He stares at her. "And could you do something else? Could you keep in mind that maybe I'm not your little boy anymore? That maybe I'm my own boy—a mean boy—meaner than you can imagine?"

"Why would you say that? I don't think you're a little boy. And I don't think you're a mean boy. And I don't want to break up. *Please,* Wayne, I'm sorry…"

Glass rattles furiously as his mother shakes the panels. "Open these cotton-pickin' doors, Wayne! Dammit, right now!"

He stares into her eyes, draws a finger across his throat. "Didn't want to miss my calls, you said. Well you sure missed one today. I think you pegged the wrong guy with the candy wrapper. I think you were aiming for Kenny all along. I think you need glasses as well as braces—"

The glass vibrates and shudders.

"Why are you doing this…?" Tears have come into her voice, so abruptly he thinks at first she's pretending—mocking him, even. *"I love you.* I'd go crazy if we broke up. Kenny's just a friend, that's all, and he's your friend, too."

"He's no friend of mine…and you're not my girl."

The pulse is pounding in his ears now, drowning out everything—the crossing bells, the sound of wheels on rails, the shaking of glass—everything, that is, except Tilly. His mother is backing slowly away from the

255

booth—looking at him in a way he has never been looked at before. There is no love in that look, no quarter.

"He is so your friend! And I *am* your girl!" She's begins crying—balling and moaning full-out. "Wayne, please..."

"Tell him to go to hell," says Kenny.

"Oh, tell him to go to hell," he mimics. "That little suck-up. Sure, I'll go to hell, just as soon as you take that ring off and burn it. Could you do that for me, Tilly? I mean, if Kenny doesn't have his finger in you?"

There is a crashing sound as his mother drives her shoulder into the door panels—causing the glass to crack in three different places—*tak, tak, tak.* The impact is so sudden, and his mother's behavior so unexpected, that he nearly drops the phone. He stares at her a moment in silence, completely dumbfounded, but is unable to withstand her gaze. He diverts his attention to the El Camino, which his father has begun pulling up to the phone booth. He can see his father clearly behind the wheel, smiling broadly, oblivious to what has occurred. One of the dogs has its forepaws on the roof and is barking incessantly. The sunlight catches the edges of the cracks in the door, causing them to glow as if made of light, fracturing his field of view, dividing everything, the car, his father, the dogs, his mother.

Tilly is sobbing now, blubbering her words so that he can't quite understand them, only the tone: *Yes,* she seems to be saying. *You were right—you are a mean boy. I was wrong about you. I give up.* "I don't ever want to hear your voice again," she says, sniveling. "Don't you ever call me agai—"

"Fuck off!"

He slams the phone down and unblocks the doors, causing his mother to spill between the panels—stumbling a little before he catches her by the shoulders. She jerks away from him as if he were a stranger, as if he were not her son at all but maybe a killer or even a rapist. "What's the hell's gotten into you?" she says. "Did you just say to her what I think you did? *Well,* did you?"

He tilts his chin, mocks her with a smile. "No, ma'am."

"Get out of the phone booth," she says. "Go to the car. And mister—wipe that stupid smile off your face."

He watches her as she heads back toward the vehicles, shaking her head, mumbling, "You try and you

257

try and you try and you try. If that's the road you're on, buster, you're on your own, believe you me...."

He starts to follow her but pauses, noticing how her shoulders slouch and how she has lost all composure, her wit, her effervescence, her grace—not lost it but had it taken—by him, her son, her youngest, her baby. He has done this to her, not a lump in her breast or Dagora-Carcinoma. And he has done it to Tilly, too. And while his mother will forgive him and even forget, Tilly will not. He knows this just as sure as he knows that everyone will die, just go away, eventually. That even if they make up—which he can't imagine they'll do—it was at this moment that the die was cast and the end made certain, whether they are reunited for only a month or endure somehow for a thousand years.

Everything shimmers through the grimy glass and the heat. The bee sting itches and burns. He peers off down the empty tracks, which lie fallow in the California sun, inert, the tops of their rails gleaming.

If that's the road you're on, buster, you're on your own, believe you me.

258

But he is the youngest, the baby, and everyone will vanish down the road before him. So he is on his own anyway.

V | Terrified and Alone

THEY GO CRUISING AROUND L.A. one final time, the Kid riding in the bed of the Camino with the dogs, his stomach boiling, his head burning, everything reminding him of Tilly, but also of Ken Goodman: past a billboard for Smokey and the Bandit from which Sally Field—who looks like Tilly—smiles at him from Burt Reynold's arms (who doesn't look like Ken but has the same shit-eating grin); past a billboard for CBS's One Day At a Time from which Valerie Bertinelli—who also looks like Tilly—smiles out at him while standing next to Snyder the Janitor (who also doesn't look like Ken but who's banging Valerie Bertinelli in real life, he bets); past Knott's Berry Farm in Buena Vista with its rollercoasters and bleeding volcano. Behind them, Sheldon is driving his Firebird as though he were Burt Reynolds, repeatedly accelerating to within yards of the Camino and then falling back, allowing other cars to fill the space. Every

259

time the Firebird is on their tail Sheldon gesticulates out his window, as if to say, Where the hell are we going? The Kid only sneers at him: he has no idea where they are going. They seem to be making a loop, if he recalls the map correctly. The map...in the phone booth.

He cannot account for his extreme behavior in the phone booth; nor does he understand exactly why or when this cynicism gripped him. It is as if a remnant of the past, something toxic and highly flammable, has re-ignited.

Beyond that he has only a vague sense that something is still coming. Either way it is all about Tilly. It is not, as Fast Eddy says, about the Girl, the Gold Watch, Everything.

It is only about the Girl. And Ken.

It isn't until they pass the La Brea Tar Pits that he is able to forget her—them—for an instant; when his mother raps on the glass between the cab and the bed, indicating he should bring his head around to her rolled-down window. He hesitates, staring at her through the glass, trying to read her intent through the watery, flowing reflections of Mexican palms and telephone poles. And though her expression is mostly stoic, there is something in her eyes that tells him everything is all right, that they will talk about the phone booth later, that nothing has changed; which is confirmed when she points at her window again impatiently, as if to say: forget it, let's get on with the trip, now get over here—which he does, muscling aside poor Rusty, who whimpers and lolls his tongue.

His mother is holding a brochure.

"That's where we'll go next time," she says, brushing the breeze-swept hair from her eyes. "La Brea..." She gestures beyond him at a cluster of buildings in a park-like setting (which reminds him a bit of Manito Park in Spokane, and of Mirror Lake), sees statuary behind ornamental steel fencing—a giant sloth, mastodons, a saber-toothed cat. The pits are like the Spokane Aquifer only filled with oil, she says. The oil bubbles to the surface and makes pools, which then get covered with dust and leafage and form tar, and because they've been doing this for tens of thousands of years there's places where everything has evaporated but a kind of clay, in which the bones of extinct animals—who got caught in the tar—are embedded. He lifts his head, trying to see the pools, but because they are too far away and the sky has begun darkening, he can only see the statues. A single fleck of rain lands on his cheek.

She tells him they'll have a chance to see something similar, but up close, when they visit Dinosaur National Monument in northern Utah. "There they've exposed an entire wall of ancient rock," she says, "and built a structure around it. Sort of like Grandpa Spitzer's basement. But within this you'll be able to see striations indicating the passage of millions of years." He faces her, compelled by this idea. She doesn't look up from the brochure. "Entire worlds lost and covered over," she says, scanning the pages. "Stacked like coffins—buried beneath ashes and dust."

It occurs to him while watching her think that he scarcely knows his mother, as a person. That she has had an entire life previous to this, and has one still—the life of her mind. It also occurs to him that, if not for her, they wouldn't have known where to go on a trip beyond Washington State, wouldn't have known about the Movieland Wax Museum or Dinosaur National Monument. He thinks of all the books and magazines in their house—*Time* and *Life, National Geographic, Natural Wonders of the World, Our Amazing World of*

262

Nature—is grateful he has such a mother, a mother who is interested in the entire world and not just one little corner of it.

Then she reaches across the bench seat and lays a hand on his father's knee, which his father covers gently with his own, and he realizes how they complement each other: she so informed about the world and he so happy just to move around in it. He can see how happy his father is—driving the Camino without a care, his eyes bright and confident, his face tanned, the black sunglasses placed jauntily on his head, his white dress shirt gleaming.

His father is like the Camino's exterior, he realizes, everything that is clean and simple and smooth. His mother is something else, something complicated. His mother is the engine and the gears, the transmission and the drivetrain. His mother is what propels his father, and everyone else, along. And yet she, too, cannot do it alone. The world is not enough. She needs to know his father and him are close; why else would she call him over to her window in spite of being angry with him, or put a hand on his father's knee in spite of being absorbed in her reading?

263

He leans against the back of the cab, thinking about it, as thunder rumbles in the distance. It's getting cold; another fleck of rain skims his face.

Because the world is not enough. Not even this one—this landscape peppered with Mexican palms and horsehead pumps (which see-saw like feeding allosaurs) and refinery towers that belch volcanic flames. This primordial country presided over by a hundred harvest moons—in the form of sunset-orange Union '76 globes, of course. None of it is enough or even particularly interesting without someone to share it with. In fact, it's all quite depressing—a Land of the Lost.

The word 'metaphor' comes to mind; but then he loses the thought amidst the roar of Sheldon's Firebird, which is tailgating again, its twin hood scoops pointed at him like weapons, his older brother smiling rakishly, insincerely, predictably.

They arrive in San Diego in time to visit Sea World and to catch Shamu the Killer Whale's last performance of the day, by which time the Kid has spent two hours riding up front with his parents and listening to the radio: to "I Will Survive" by Donna Summer and "Tragedy" by the Bee Gees and "Do Ya Think I'm Sexy" by Rod

Stewart, which has put him into an even deeper funk than when they left Los Angeles. He resolves while watching dolphins leap before a mock volcano that he will call Tilly again when they get to Las Vegas, that he will throw himself at her mercy and beg for forgiveness; that he doesn't care if Ken Goodman was in her house or even if he still is; he loves her more than anything and knows that she loves him, and knows also that he can't possibly go on without her—that without her he is less than nothing, will never be well or sane or even human, only trembling, terrified, alone.

VI | The Arm of the Milky Way

SHE BREAKS INTO TEARS the instant she hears his voice, crying so intensely and for so long that he is stunned speechless, can hardly believe that any human being, much less the prettiest girl at North Pines—though only he and Ken Goodman have apprehended it, a beauty so quiet and obvious one might see through it like water—could be moved so much by him, a skinny boy with stringy hair whom a bully once said looked like a white rat. He isn't sure how it makes him feel, her crying

265

and moaning because of him, other than needed, vital, imperative, as though he is oxygen itself and so must be protected, provided for, kept close. He lets her cry for a long time even though his parents think he is using Circus-Circus's restroom. In fact he has ducked into a phone booth in the lobby, a booth with a window looking out on the Strip, on Freemont Avenue, on the Golden Nugget Casino and the Gold Rush Hotel, on the giant neon cowboy destroyed by Glen Langan as *The Colossal Man,* everything flashing and glittering to the tune of "Too Much Heaven" by the Bee Gees—which Tilly is playing on her turntable.

"I love you, Wayne," she says softly, her voice wavering, cracking a little. "I hope we never break up because I'd go crazy. I did go crazy, when you told me to take the dollar ring off and throw it away." She laughs. "Now it's in the bushes somewhere. I don't want Kenny. I want you. I've always wanted you, since the moment I saw you. Please believe me, Wayne. I've never, ever felt this way, not about anyone."

And he does believe her—perhaps for the very first time. It seems clear to him now that this was necessary somehow; that without this incident and without this pain they could not have come to where they are now, which is entirely different from where they were before. Now he feels as though they have been cradled in the hand of something black and hard and vast, like a mountain. Something with ducts through which cold water flows, which rests beneath a mantle of silence and snow, which is heated from below as if by a furnace drawing slow, mighty breaths and blowing warm air through everything.

"I love you, too, Tilly."

And that is the extent of the conversation, those sentiments repeated over and over as Tilly puts the phone down sporadically and changes '45s, as the long-distance bill grows somewhere out of sight—doubling and redoubling and tripling, he knows—but doesn't care, because this is all that matters, and they are rich now anyway, his family. They can afford it.

THE ONLY THING LEFT of the farmhouse his mother grew up in is a crudely-poured foundation and a cellar that has been filled with debris, although she discovers a decaying baby doll nearby whose head has been chewed nearly in half. She thinks the doll belonged to her as a

267

child, or perhaps her sister, but cannot be sure. All the Kid knows is that it would make a great prop for a horror movie. He volunteers to take it back to the car while his parents scour the rest of the area with flashlights.

They are alone in the high desert about ten miles south of Moab, pulled off to the side of US Route 160, not far from the Colorado River. Sheldon and John have gone ahead of them in the Firebird to "reserve a motel"—which the Kid finds ludicrous. Who else on earth is out here besides them?

He examines the doll by moonlight, wondering what his mother could see in it now that it is so old and filthy and ruined. Perhaps it is a reminder of Kim—who would have been his middle brother—who died in childbirth. It is obvious to him that Kim is still with her—them—in every way. Why else would they have purchased a plot at Greenwood Cemetery, even had a marker made, and insist they lay flowers upon it every Memorial Day? He gazes back at his parents, who have reconvened at the cellar's edge, his father putting an arm around his mother's shoulders, the beams of their flashlights vanishing into the hole. They make quite an image, really, his mother and father, so small against the stars

268

and the horizon, the sandstone mesas, the yucca plants and Joshua trees. He wonders if he and Tilly will ever make such an image, or have and lose a son. He wonders if Kim has anything to do with it at all, this staring into the cellar, this fascination and reverence for what appears to be just a hole in the ground. He reaches into the Camino and lays the doll on the dash; he has to pee, and with all this moonlight and starlight he doesn't want to be seen by his parents, who are only about fifty feet away.

He climbs a slope on the other side of the road and descends its opposite bank, thinking about Tilly, about her chestnut-brown hair and gap-toothed smile, her pixie-like face which he can hold like a cup, and about her body, most of which he has not seen but some of which he has, like her legs, which are perfectly formed because she is slim and short, and her neck and collarbone, and her belly and shoulders which he has seen only once, when she wore the shirred elastic tube top that reminded him of the striped rag rug his mother used to cover the phone cord in the kitchen with.

He takes *it* out, becoming aware of the conflict inherent in having to pee while thinking about Tilly,

269

moving his feet apart to steady himself on the slope, waiting for the plumbing to sort itself, tightening his stomach, giving the process a little push, until his urine arcs across the sand and he looks at the sky, shaking the hair from his eyes, and realizes what his mother meant when she said that seeing the stars from the desert wasn't like seeing them from Spokane, "where there's so much light pollution," but more like seeing them from outer space, and that he'd recognize the stars were not in fact individual lights but light itself—the entire galaxy, the Milky Way. And staring at the sky he sees this is so: sees the Milky Way with its arm spread across the night, sheltering him as he pees but also sheltering Tilly in Spokane, his parents out in the field, Sheldon and John on their way to Moab, everything.

VII | The Willows

THEY ARE SLOW-DANCING TOO FAST, he knows. In fact, they are completely out of beat. He supposes he should take the lead and slow things down, but he doesn't want to, not today. Tilly's mother has had to take a second job because of the recession, and will not be

270

home until 7:30 P.M.; so they have made plans to walk together to her place after the dance—where, because Tilly's little sister is staying with her grandmother, they will have the apartment to themselves. If, by some chance, her mother comes home early, they have an alibi. They will tell her he was there to help her find the dollar ring; which Tilly has searched for—in vain—for over a month.

Because they are in middle school the dance is occurring in the afternoon rather than the evening, and is strictly casual. It is being held to celebrate everyone's return for the 1979-1980 school year, in the gymnasium, and most everyone is there, including the Two Ks, Kevin Franklin, of course, but also Ken Goodman—whom, based upon Tilly's urging, the Kid has continued an uneasy friendship with. At least one of the kid's bullies is there, too: Keith Warren, who once mocked him for drawing the *U.S.S. Enterprise* on the chalkboard in 1st grade, and now mocks him for slow-dancing too fast, although Keith himself keeps stepping on his dance partner's feet. Still, it isn't Warren's gaze he keeps meeting over Tilly's shoulder, but Ken's, who seems more interested in what he and Tilly are doing than what

271

he is doing with his own partner, a cheerleader named Holly.

As for Tilly, she has begun to grow her hair so that it falls below her shoulders and swings, shining, whenever she turns her head, and although she has not yet started wearing makeup—and still appears relatively boyish—he has begun to notice how all the guys look at her, not just her face and hair but everything, for she has filled out some, and though they smile sheepishly when she sees them, or deferentially when they see him, he knows what they are thinking, knows about their weasel designs and what they would try, like pickpockets in a crowd, were he distracted. But he has not been distracted, not since returning from Southern California. He has focused on Tilly to the exclusion of all else—most notably school, which he knows he will never need. Sheldon has already begun painting with their father part-time for sixteen dollars an hour; he will do the same—while continuing to write his fiction and plan his movies. Eventually he will take her away from Spokane to L.A. or to New York.

Tilly lives on Alki Street, which is nearly as far east as the Kid's house is north, so they have plenty of time to flirt and knock hips together as they walk along the

272

road's edge—a rush of cool air ruffling his white Star Wars T-shirt and causing Tilly's black windbreaker to undulate. They walk with their arms around each other's shoulders until they pass a maroon-colored convalescence center—which Tilly says marks the half-way point—where he slides his hand down and hooks a thumb into the back pocket of her blue jeans. She responds by laying her head on his shoulder, saying *"Mmmm"*—causing his groin to tighten fiercely, so much that he begins to wonder what will happen when they reach her apartment, and if he is ready for it. Regardless, *something* is going to happen. He knows this just as he knew he was being invited into a ritual when she started throwing the candy wrappers at the pep rally last year; even as he knew his mother was probably right when she said that everything was proceeding too fast between them, that they were not mature enough to be so emotionally involved or even going steady—but it is too late. The ritual is underway.

Yet there is a complication. Tilly's little sister, Tawny, is in fact home; her grandmother has dropped her off early—the reason for which he doesn't hear, because he knows Tilly's mother would never allow boys in her room and knows also the little sister will tell, and so is already thinking about alternatives, coming up with nothing. He waits while the sisters sequester themselves in Tawny's room, whispering conspiratorially, heatedly, as though they are bartering, which he supposes they are.

Because they have not lived long in the apartment, there isn't much to look at while he waits, other than a painting on black velvet of Burt Reynolds—which Tilly's mother has hung over the fireplace—who looks at him with the same shit-eating grin as he did from the billboard in L.A.; but who is completely naked and sprawled across a bear rug, his arm blocking his privates—mostly—and a cigarette dangling from his mouth. It's a ridiculous picture—a ridiculous subject in a ridiculous form—yet there is something threatening about it; something about the shit-eating grin, which reminds him of Ken Goodman—and of Sheldon, too— something which reminds him of his panic attack at the East Sprague Drive-in Theater and of Fast Eddy's demonic sublime. Maybe it's all that hair, the thick mustache, the forests of black ringlets that cover his chest and arms and stomach and legs, the bear rug. He wonders if he'll ever look like that, like Bionic Bigfoot

274

from *The Six Million Dollar Man,* and if that's desirable to every woman or just some. Mostly he wonders if it's desirable to Tilly.

The door to Tawny's room slams—so violently it makes him jump—and Tilly storms past—taking his hand, saying, "Come on, Wayne."

She leads him out the sliding glass door to the back porch and down the community lawn, to where a hedgerow of willow bushes separates the apartment grounds from a massive, fenced-in power station. The clouds have piled high and it has begun to sprinkle as they step into the shrubs, poking and feeling their way through the thickets until arriving at a rock the size of an end table, which lays hidden in the bushes like a tumor. They sit upon it still holding hands, angling their bodies to face each other.

"Wow," says the Kid, looking around the little clearing. "Is this where you lost the—"

She cups his mouth. "Grandma didn't know about the dance and so assumed I'd be home to babysit. Tawny, of course, called Mom, who left work early and is on her way here." She lowers her chin, looks sharply into his eyes. "The good news is she works in Medical Lake. You should kiss me now, Wayne."

The wind gusts as he looks at her, blowing her chestnut hair sideways across her face, causing the willow bushes to lean and their branches to sway and their silvery leaves to rattle. He leans toward her but pauses—thinking about Hedy Lamarr and Robert Taylor—then pulls her against him, kissing her the way people in movies and on TV kiss—seriously, intently, like Captain James T. Kirk (the living one not the wax one), as wind blows and rain sprinkles and the power station hums. She kisses him back, running her hands through his hair, making *Mmmm*-ing sounds, probing his mouth with her tongue. He continues to kiss her, liking the kissing but using it really only to keep the circuit open—the current flowing—while he works his hand into her pants; while he strains and gropes, his fingertips entering a lattice of thread—tough, wiry thread, like un-spooled fishing line—which he takes at first to be the fraying cotton of her panties but quickly realizes is no such thing.

He finds this startling, terrifying—that her body should be so developed, so adult-like, while his remains

276

smooth and bare, like a child's. He looks over her shoulder at the tangled, crisscrossed branches, their leaves shot through with gray-green light (because they have not yet turned), and it appears to him for a moment that he and Tilly are inhabiting more than just a stand of willow bushes, but a place somehow both skeletal and ghostly. A place comprised of individual parts yet surrounded by pure energy. Then she places her hand on the crouch of his jeans and he loses the thought, loses everything save the warmth and smell of her. And when he looks over her shoulder again it is only to scan the bramble for the lost dollar ring.

THE YELLOW JACKETS go and come again as 1979 becomes 1980. The trees shed their leaves and re-bloom. The world beyond Spokane intrudes more and more each month via television and radio. In Iran, a country the Kid has never even heard of, thousands of students storm the U.S. Embassy in Tehran and take 90 hostages, mostly Americans. Ronald Reagan, the Governor of California, announces he will run for President of the United States. He does this on national television while pointing at a globe of the world, suggesting that Americans are at a turning point and urging them to keep their "rendezvous with destiny." The Kid's mother can only shake her head, repeating, "That man will get us into World War III."

And *Star Trek: The Motion Picture* makes its local premiere at the Fox Theater in downtown Spokane, which the Kid sees with his friend Kevin Franklin, and which causes them to argue bitterly afterward, Kevin having loved it but the Kid having reservations, arguing that the pacing was slow and the emphasis on special effects too great. And thus they see less and less of each other as the months fly past—*bang, bang, bang,* like that.

VIII | The Auto Shop

SHE IS JUST ABOUT TO COME, he is sure of it, when he hears a vehicle pull up and honk. They are in the evergreen bushes which separate Tilly's apartment complex from the power station. It is April 22, 1980, Tilly's 16th birthday, and they have just gotten back from watching John Frankenheimer's *Prophecy: The Monster Movie* at the Fox Theater in downtown Spokane. He ignores it at first, continuing to kiss her and to wiggle his finger, wanting desperately to please her; but gives up

278

on the fourth honk, fearing that her mother, hearing the commotion, will come searching. Tilly steps into her panties and hitches them up beneath her dress as he peers between the branches—sees his father's work truck parked at the curb in the gray late-afternoon drizzle. Something about the image reminds him that something important was to take place today, although he has no idea at present what that thing was, nor why the sight of his father's truck should make him think of it.

Fast Eddy sings as they approach, "Here she *commmes,* Miss *Amaaarica…*" which causes Tilly to laugh through her nose and cover her face and start to turn away before the Kid pulls her back by her fingertips. "Tilly," he says, "meet Fast Eddy. Fast Eddy…Tilly." Fast Eddy taps ashes on the lawn and sticks his cigarette in his mouth, extends his hand which is covered in paint. "Please to meet you Miss Tilly. I think it would be fair to say I've heard something about you."

She shakes his hand. "Nice to finally meet you, Fast Eddy. How are you, Mr. Spitzer?"

The Kid looks at his father, who looks even more exhausted than usual. His eyes are red as though he has been drinking. "Hi there," says his father, and clears his throat. "Hi there."

"Tell Bozo here to call me before he goes to bed," she says, squeezing the Kid's hand, then turns and heads toward her apartment.

He climbs in as Eddy slides over, slams the door. "What's going on, Dad?"

"We're going to check on the Camino," says Fast Eddy, and takes a sip of his beer. "It had to go into the shop."

"Right on..." He waves at Tilly as they pull from the curb. "What's wrong with it?"

Fast Eddy takes a drag off his cigarette, blows blue smoke from his nostrils. "They said they'd explain it when we got there."

HE THINKS ABOUT *PROPHECY: THE MONSTER MOVIE* as they drive to Benny's Car Clinic in north Spokane, the rain picking up, the Chevy's windshield wipers clicking in lockstep; and about one scene in particular, which has been branded on his memory not only because it was shocking but because they were high in the balcony and Tilly had wrapped her fingers about him and was moving her hand up and down—but stopped because the scene startled her. Nor did they return to making out and fondling each other afterward, but remained wholly concentrated on the movie until the very end. In the scene a doctor played by Robert Foxworth has just shown a lumber mill director a deformed bear cub—"The result," he says, "of Methyl-Mercury spilling out of your plant"—who flees the tent in horror only to be pursued by the doctor, who keeps repeating, *"Did you know?"* When the lumber mill director confesses, "I didn't want to…" the conversation is interrupted by a fur-covered shape moving through the pines—a shape everyone fears is Mother Bear, also deformed, or "Katahdin," the "Monster" of the title—but which turns out only to be the wise old Indian, M'Rai, at which point everyone breathes a sigh of relief.

But the breath has hardly escaped everyone's lungs when Katahdin herself bursts through the trees—pushing the trunks over and spilling fuel drums and swatting aside the evil paper mill employees and valiant Indians alike, one of whom falls across the campfire and bursts into flame—which spreads to the spilt gasoline and races along it, causing a nearby jeep to explode and everyone

281

to flee, screaming. This is precisely how horror movies work, he realizes, as they pull into the dirt lot of Benny's Car Clinic, and splash through the potholes. They get you on the rebound, on the exhale, on the sigh of relief. It is how they access you and make you do what they want— how they put you on the ride. It is the dark spot beneath their garments; their ticket-taker at Disneyland, their demonic sublime.

He walks through the rain and into the office behind his father and Fast Eddy, who pats his father on the back, which the Kid finds odd. There are others seated in the waiting area, like patients in an emergency room. His father and Fast Eddy approach the counter. "Hi there," says his father to a man with a clipboard, and clears his throat. "Hi there."

"We're here for the El Camino," says Fast Eddy.

"The Camino…that's Roddy." The man circles around the counter and opens a door. "Follow me."

The Kid follows them into a cavernous work area with a vaulted metal ceiling that is suffused with a limbo-like light—the result of cloudy skylights mixed with suspended banks of sterile white fluorescents—and which echoes with the sounds of clanging tools and

282

torque wrenches. The shop is bigger than he realized, having never been inside and having paid little attention to the exterior, opening onto chambers beyond the immediate one—all of them lined with big, red Rotary Lifts with levers on their sides and hydraulic cables and ventricle-like hoses suspended in giant 'S's, like monstrous black adders—the maroon-painted heating and air-conditioning ducts exposed and suspended from long rods so that it feels to the Kid as though they are moving through a gargantuan human heart. He looks from side to side as they walk down the central aisle flanked by cars and trucks in various states of repair, chromed tools scattered haphazardly across their fenders like surgical implements. "Right down here," says the man leading them, as they clomp over grates in the floor under which something like kitchen grease can be seen (like the kind his mother keeps in a cup atop the stove), and which make him think of the La Brea tar Pits, so that he half expects a mucosal eye to open and blink at him through the grill, like a lesser Dagora-Carcinoma, the one of gas-stations and repair shops.

He glimpses the Camino between the backs of his father and Fast Eddy before Eddy touches his father

283

again, this time on the shoulder—blocking his line of site so that he has to step to one side, where he sees the El Camino in the last stall on the right, unwashed, filthy, barely recognizable in the funereal glow of the skylights and fluorescents—its hood propped open and its fenders draped with paper mats the color of surgeons' scrubs. There are greasy black smudges all down its side and its roof is cluttered with socket wrenches and pans of fluid, a snuff-caked spittoon, oily rags. Little grilled work-lights with hooks on them hang everywhere; so do long, pale-red tubes (used to supply compressed air to the power tools), which dangle from big red-black spindles near the ceiling, the roof of which is being pelted by rain, which sluices along the gutters and trickles down drainpipes and drips winding down the shop's tall windows, casting the shadows of rivulets on a massive dryer hose—which extends from the wall and hangs slanting to the Camino's tailpipe, like an intravenous feeding tube. Someone—presumably Roddy—says, "I'm afraid it's about as bad as it could be, Mr. Spitzer...."

He circles the car slowly, noticing for the first time how scratched and pitted it is, how bald the tires are, how the dent Sheldon put in the rear quarter panel has rusted,

284

just as his father said it would. He peers into the cab through the passenger-side door, which is hanging open, sees that they have removed the cowl and housing from around the gearshift and exposed the greasy black interior of the transmission hump. He imagines that the carpet itself has been torn up and clamped back with cold instruments, that the flooring has been ripped apart and the mound itself cut open, like a fish, and that he can see right through it, to a red-black hell of saw-edged wheels and bitter teeth—the Camino's demonic sublime; the brutal machinery of the universe, Dagora-Carcinoma, Time and Death. And it is as though nothing has ever existed but the car, this machine which has carried him through his entire boyhood—from 1972 into 1980, more than half his life—nothing but it and the rustle of the roll-up doors in the wind.

And he remembers, quite suddenly, what important thing was to happen today, for he remembers his mother was to have a doctor's appointment. That they had found something of concern.

"…you might get three more years out of her, tops," says Roddy, "with a new transmission and an engine rebuild. Failing that, I can get her running temporarily, but not for long, and not well. Watch that tranny fluid…"

The Kid looks down to find himself standing in a puddle of red-black liquid, which has spread over the floor like a cloud of spilt ink, which has been smeared and tracked across the concrete as at a murder scene, and to his father, who looks back at him and tries to smile, sweetly, wanly—not, the Kid realizes, as if he has been drinking, but as if he has been crying, trembling. As if he has been taken for a ride through the monolith—like the astronaut David Bowman—and aged a thousand years. And finally he looks at the dashboard, where he sees his mother's Bible, which is wedged against the windshield, the cracks in which have spread, dividing and re-dividing, to every part of the glass.

IX | The Fall

HE HAS DECIDED, after the events of the last few months, to become a kid again. Has decided it in the face of the return of his mother's cancer and the seeing of a dollar ring on Kenny's finger (who *saw* him seeing, and smiled his shit-eating grin). He has decided it in the face

286

of his failing grades and the look in Tilly's eyes when he mentioned to her what a coincidence it was that Kenny should have a ring just like the one she'd lost in the bushes—the bushes she had led him to that day, although he hadn't thought anything of it at the time, so swiftly and assuredly, as though she had already known there was a private oasis inside. As though she had been there before—with Kenny. With *someone.*

He has decided it in the face of a film shown in class about jellyfish and Man o' Wars, and how, if not killed, they can, in theory, live indefinitely. That Dagora-Carcinoma is a kind of Man o' War, and has been all along; that his great, billowing body and dangling tentacles are but the features of an immortal creature whose respiration propels it through the water...even as the pistons of the Camino's engines have propelled him through the years.

He has decided, at last, that there is no death and thus nothing to fear. That there is only combustion and respiration. That all creation is alive and that what we think of as birth and death is only the universe itself breathing. And he has decided that, this being the case,

287

his mother shall never truly die…nor he grow into an adult.

For he is—and will remain—the X-Ray Rider. And now that school is out he is running—running like a little boy—for home; even as lightning flashes in the blue-black sky and splinters it into a thousand shards, until at last he sees the back of their house about a half-mile north—and, seeking a shortcut, swerves into someone's yard.

There is a narrow concrete path along the side of this house, its surface soaking wet so that it reflects track lights embedded in the eaves. Its perimeter is guarded by an iron rail. He vaults over the rail—*More than human! More than divine! X-Ray Rider! X-Ray Runner!*—but there is no concrete, no reflection. He is falling, arms swinging….

HE IS LYING AT THE BOTTOM of a stairwell. There is broken glass everywhere as if he has fallen through a window, which he has, or at least the glass portion of a basement door, which stands ajar, creaking. He vaguely recalls hearing sheets of paper swish-swishing down, scattering around him. He is bleeding from his palms, his

288

head, his nose, his arms—one of which is numb, sleeping. He feels himself all over with his good hand, expecting brains to be oozing out, bones protruding. But nothing seems to be broken, although his left leg is splayed uncomfortably. Glass grates as he grips his ankle, pulling it toward him, dragging papers along, and folds it beneath him. He tries to stand but there is nothing to grip, only the door pane which is spiked with glass. His head swims dizzily. How could he be so stupid? Falling for such an obvious illusion—mistaking the shining wet stairwell and the light above its door for a reflection. The thought of it shames him.

He hears something pattering against the windbreaker—blood from his nose, blotting the powder-blue nylon with splotches of maroon.

He looks at the top of the well, a concrete rectangle with the dimensions of a tomb, sees darkened eaves, hazily, and beyond them, storm clouds, drifting across the sky. He places his good hand against the wall and climbs to his knees, not wanting to remain in the stairwell another instant, wanting to run home as fast as he can, to his mother and bedroom and plastic model kits, to beige-colored carpets and warm air blowing from heat registers. The concrete wall of the well presses bitter cold against his palm.

He crawls upon his knees through the broken glass, gathering up pages, smearing them with blood. When he gets them back into the folder he staggers out of the stairwell, one landing at a time, his injured leg resisting, but feels a wave of nausea as he reaches the top—and pivots, so that he is leaning against the rail, staring into the well, breathing heavily.

The broken door below sways and creaks. The rain drones against the world.

This is what it will *actually* be like, he thinks, when they lower her into the vault. As he and his brothers—pallbearers, if episodes of *Night Gallery* are any indication—stand brooding. As his father stands off to one side looking like the widows in movies, only minus the veil—glassy-eyed, untouchable, waltzing with ghosts. As the minister takes a handful of earth and shakes it onto the casket, saying, 'Ashes to ashes, dust to dust...' Until the caretakers come and begin shoveling dirt into her eyes. And she will begin sobbing because it is cold down there and she is so alone, abandoned by everyone. Because she was a good wife and a good mother and it all ends like this, with shovelfuls of earth in her eyes and hair.

HE RUNS, LIMPING, through the sodden fields—sliding upon his back beneath the Meyers' electric fence, which he touches in spite of everything, fingertips burning, blistering up—staggering over chunks of masonry—"The Rock Pile" his brother used to call it, that reef of boulders and debris separating their property from the neighbors', like an asteroid belt or demilitarized zone, Central Front in the Cold War Between Kids, most of whom have moved away.

He runs and runs, leaving a trail of blood, until he bangs through the kitchen door and on into the dining room, bringing a gust of wind—which riffles the papers stacked all along the table—stacks and stacks of paper—the top sheets of which take flight and see-saw back down, going *swish-swish*. He has not even had time to call out to his mother when something hits the house with a violent thud—causing him to jump and the very floor to vibrate, as if a comet has slammed into the earth. He looks around the room; the house is silent except for a muted, sputtering rumble, which is coming from outside.

291

He goes to the window and sees the Camino swinging into the field next to the station wagon. There's a new dent in its rear quarter-panel, severe enough that the taillight has been smashed and the chromed El Camino indicia dangles, swinging back and forth. He feels his nose dripping and looks down, sees blood dotting the beige shag carpet.

He hobbles out as his mother puts the car into park—sees a hole the size of a milk crate taken from the corner of the house, chunks of cinderblock littering the drive.

"I—I was backing up to the breezeway," she says, gasping, jogging toward him. "To unload the groceries. I—*what happened to you?!*"

He looks from the broken cinderblocks to his mother, who pauses in the drive, as if to confirm what she is seeing. She seems mighty as Chief Seattle to him in that moment, fierce, wizened, but vulnerable too, frail—not from age but something else, something which has weaved itself into her fiber and begun betraying her, betraying him, as a threat from without could never have done. For she is the strength, the rock, and when she is gone there will be no justice, not for him, who is

292

inherently weak, and not for his father, who is the same. Everything is owed her, he sees suddenly, his lower lip trembling. Everything is owed her and nothing can be repaid.

He rushes to her and throws his arms about her, will not let go no matter how much she insists, no matter how much she wants to look at his nose, his forehead, his arms. He squeezes her as hard as he can, his cheek pressed against her blouse—which becomes smeared with blood—breathing her in, feeling her breath. He imagines her smiling down at him, the way she did when he was a baby, lying in a wash basin, being bathed by her. When her hair was thick and wavy and honey-blonde—her skin tanned, her teeth white. Back before her hair was so thin and brittle and shot through with gray.

He looks at the El Camino, and behind it, at the gaping crater left in the house. And he realizes in that instant that his mother was wrong about the dinosaurs, that they became extinct because they couldn't adapt. After all, everyone knew better now. No, they became instinct because of a giant rock straight out of nowhere. They became extinct because something from the heart

293

of the universe had reached across the light-years and smote them once and for all time.

SHE IS MOPPING HIS FACE with a moistened dishrag, dabbing at his temples, swabbing out his ears. He sits facing opposite the dinner table with a towel draped over his shoulders and another over his lap. She has cleaned and dressed his wounds and even trimmed his hair—but left it mostly long, at his insistence, so that it still falls below his shoulders, because he will need it that way in High School.

When she has finished she tells him to turn his chair around and to disregard all the papers, which clutter the table. What he needs now, she says, is soup, which she has simmering. He scans the tabletop as she fetches him a bowl and finds there is a little bit of everything—bills marked Sacred Heart Medical Center and Deaconess Hospital and Inland Imaging, forms marked Chapter 11 Bankruptcy, bids for jobs—small ones, by the looks of it, convenience stores and private homes. Mostly there are the bills—bills with long numbers printed on them and 'PAST DUE' stamped across the top—piles and piles of them.

294

"Mom," he says, watching her busy herself about the kitchen, watching her busy herself and busy herself. She goes to pour him a glass of milk but realizes there is none, at least not in the refrigerator. Everything is still in the car, she says. A gallon of milk, plus potatoes and hamburger-helper, for dinner. And a quart of ice cream, for desert. She starts putting on her old fuzzy coat, the one with the frayed cuffs and the hole in the elbow, to go out to the car. "Mom," he says again. "Please. Sit."

She looks at him as though she has been slapped, but sits, tentatively, guardedly. "Okay, but wear a coat." She rubs her upper arms, shivering a little. But it isn't cold, not with the heat pumping through the registers and the doors sensibly shut and all the windows closed.

He limps out to the Camino in only his tennis shoes, jeans, and T-shirt. The storm has passed, leaving everything clean and wet and still. The driver's door groans as he swings it open—sees the paper bag full of groceries lying on the floor, leaning against the transmission hump, the ice cream melted, staining the carpet. Because the keys are still in the ignition the warning indicator goes *ding, ding, ding.*

295

His father's work truck pulls into the concrete driveway, its breaks squealing as he rolls up to the house. The Kid waits and waits for his father to get out, wondering why it is taking him so long, what is he doing, besides just sitting there, his hands on the wheel, staring straight ahead, staring through the windshield. Then his mother comes out in her fuzzy coat and helps him from the cab, supports him with an arm around his waist, limps with him into the breezeway and away from view.

The Kid leans in and picks up the bag, the center of which does not hold, spilling the soggy carton of ice cream and the gallon of milk and the boxes of hamburger-helper all over the floor. He stares at the mess feeling suddenly tired, wondering if this is how his parents always feel, and about the costs of things— wishing they could just go for a ride. That they could just go and never come back. That they could just ride on like this forever, never running out of gas, never running out of road. Then he picks up the hamburger-helper and the gallon of milk, pulls the keys from the ignition, and slams the door.

Bang, bang, bang, like that.

296

HE IS LAYING ON THE GRASS beneath the projector's beam just outside the concessions bar, his head propped against his wadded-up jacket, watching a blonde boy running through a field in which everything is painted redden-gold by the setting sun, which flares off the lens and makes multicolored circles.

They are celebrating his fifteenth birthday, he and his parents, at the West-end Drive-in, where *The Land That Time Forgot* is playing with *The Legend of Boggy Creek,* which no one minds seeing again. It is a new world in which he turns fifteen, a new country. Ronald Reagan has become President of the United States and *The Empire Strikes Back* has been in theaters for over a year—indoor multiplexes mostly, because the Drive-ins are dying, the victims of higher rental fees (due to mega-blockbusters like *The Empire Strikes Back*) and skyrocketing land values. It is a new Spokane also—the old one having witnessed a cloud of volcanic ash spread silently across its horizon; as though Mount Saint Helens had not just erupted but been murdered and was bleeding, burying everything, making a moonscape—

297

which the Kid and his parents bounced gleefully across in the dented old Camino; driving to the top of Mount Spokane and sitting on the hood, where they watched the pastel-gray sky falling and his mother held her head back, smiling at the ashes, welcoming them, absently petting Ginger, who had recently given birth to puppies, all of them full-sized now.

He looks at the projection beam, not one beam but many, like a prism, full of smaller beams, rising and falling, flickering like flames, like fire, eternal, uncreated—knowing even if they went out, if every light in Spokane went out, there would still be the Milky Way, although he wouldn't be able to see it, not through the cloud wrack and surrounding light pollution. He thinks about Tilly, whom he has long since broken up with, who has in fact not gone 'crazy' but is dating a football player at University High School. He thinks about Sheldon, who has begun college at nearby Eastern Washington University, but whom he has not spoken to since their mother's diagnosis of metastatic breast cancer—which has spread to the bone marrow and cannot be cured. He thinks about his father, who has begun spending time in Hillyard again. And he thinks about Lori, whom he has

298

met at a kegger, who has a long face and a long body and wears too much blue eye shadow.

He has no idea how he and his father will manage all the dogs or how they will manage the painting business or what they will do about the IRS, which has decided to audit them. He supposes he will just do his best to feed and water them, as he fed and watered his salamander, the one given him by Fast Eddy, but which leapt from his hand one day and escaped into the field—where he later found its delicate, bleached bones. He found them during the Mt. Saint Helens clean-up, while helping his father and Eddy limb the big willow tree, the roots of which had been threatening the house, like Dagora-Carcinoma's tentacles, until they wedged and dropped the entire trunk so that it fell like a sword between the green backyard—in which the battered Camino sat, shining, for he'd washed it himself—and the deaden weeds, at which point they soaked it in gasoline because it was too big to move, and burned it where it lay.

And finally, before beginning to nod off, he thinks of Dagora-Carcinoma—not as an all-consuming monster but as a great jellyfish or Man o' War, ancient and immortal, undulating through whatever void lay beyond

299

the cosmos itself, its body comprised of everything that ever was and could ever be, and its respiration that of the same.

When he sleeps he dreams of ash. Ash falling like snow, like leaves, trapping his mother and Spokane and the 1970s he knew, preserving them in tar. Ash falling on drive-in theater marquees and the orange globes of Union 76 stations. On traffic lights and rock quarries and Chinese restaurants. Ash falling on his mother and father and brother and himself; and on all the young and old who ever were or will be, stacking them like sheets of paper, like the papery layers of a wasp's nest, or the striations of rock in the California desert.

The End

Printed in Great Britain
by Amazon

30253754R00171